# BEST YOU EVER HAD

## MONICA WALTERS

B. Love Publications

# INTRODUCTION

Hello, Readers!

Thank you for purchasing and/or downloading this book. This work of art contains explicit sex scenes, physical abuse of an elderly person, moments of depression, and some violence. This is also somewhat of an insta-love story. You'll understand what I mean if you choose to continue. It's also a little more urban than what you may be used to from me, but it doesn't overpower the romance.

If any of the above mentioned offend you or serve as triggers for unpleasant times, please do not read.

Also, please remember that your reality isn't everyone's reality. What may seem unrealistic to you could be very real for someone else. But also keep in mind that this is a fictional story.

If you are okay with the previously mentioned warnings, I hope that you enjoy the read.

Monica

## C olson

*"WELL, GOT DAMN. I'LL BE HER SUGAR ZADDY ANY DAY OF THE week."*

It was a good decision to meet with investors and my marketing team during spring break in Galveston, Texas. The pickings were ripe, and I was ready to eat. This thick-ass lil mama was calling out to me. The way she swayed her hips to the music in this sports bar was wearing me down fast. It had been a while since I'd had time to engage in extracurricular activities, so it was long overdue. Working hard to maintain my chain of Smoothie Kings and my couple of high-end furniture stores, I could use a break.

I'd just started yet another Smoothie King here in Galveston that I planned to drop in on tomorrow. But tonight... I felt like having fun... taking a risk... getting my dick wet. The young tenderoni I was looking at would be just my speed. Her jeans looked to be painted on her, giving me the perfect view of all that body she was hauling around. Her top was less revealing. It was a black V-neck that seemed to tie at her waist. Sipping my drink, I continued to watch her, caressing her every curve with my gaze. She didn't look to be over thirty, but I didn't mind. Just so long as she wasn't under twenty-one. Continuing to watch her, I barely noticed the woman sitting next to me. She cleared her throat and said, "Hello."

"Hello, beautiful."

Yes, I was a flirt. She blushed under my gaze as I smiled at her, and then I turned my attention back to lil mama, dancing with her friends. She spun around, laughing, and her eyes fell right on mine. She held my gaze for a moment, then turned away. *Uh huh. I was gonna have her eventually.* As "How Many Drinks" by Miguel started to play, I wondered the same thing about my new obsession. Bringing my attention back to the woman sitting next to me, I asked, "What's your name?"

"Charli. And yours?" she asked as she slid her hand in mine.

"Colson. Nice to meet you. Are you from here?"

"Actually, yes. You can't be from the island, though. I would have made your acquaintance before now."

I smiled. She was a little too sure of herself. While I was naturally a flirt, Charli didn't do anything for me. I called her beautiful simply out of habit. She wasn't ugly, but she wasn't my type, I supposed. I liked my women with a little meat on their bones, that could dress to the nines and even when they dressed down, they still looked amazing. Like the goddess on the makeshift dancefloor. Charli scanned me from my baldhead, to the tattoo on my neck, then further south to my white shirt and gray slacks.

I supposed I was giving off a vibe that said I wasn't interested, because she suddenly got up and left with another man. Good riddance. I glanced at the young woman again, to find her staring at me. After settling my tab, I could see her friends pushing her in my direction. She would have never approached me otherwise. *I liked that*. I was old school in a sense. Being the aggressor turned me on. She sat next to me at the bar as I stared at her. I could tell she was extremely uncomfortable, so I tried to ease her nerves a bit. "Hi, I'm Colson. You ladies look to be enjoying yourselves tonight."

She smiled and took my hand. Everything that was lacking with Charli was definitely there with her. It was like sparks flew before she even opened her mouth. She smiled and said, "Hi. I'm Sky. We are. We're here to enjoy spring break and... umm... they seemed to think that I should approach you. This isn't something that I normally do."

"Don't worry. I can tell you're uncomfortable. But there's no need to be. You're a beautiful woman."

Her eyes widened somewhat as if she either didn't think she was beautiful, or she was surprised I said so. "Thank you."

As the DJ played a rap track by who I recognized as Dave East, I asked her, "Where are you from?"

"Beaumont. What about you?"

"Is that right? I'm originally from Port Arthur, but I live in Houston now."

"Oh wow. Small world, huh?"

"Yep. You want something to drink?"

"No. I believe I've had one too many already. Otherwise, there wouldn't have been a thing they could have said or done to convince me to come over here."

She giggled and was standing to walk away as I grabbed her hand. "Well, I'm glad you've had a drink too many."

I wanted to reiterate Miguel's sentiments from earlier, but I could tell that she would definitely shoot me down. "How long will you be on the island?"

"We're leaving Saturday. So, in three days."

"Mm. Can I see you again?"

"I don't know about that."

"Well, take my business card. If you change your mind, just call me."

She slid it from my fingertips, then stared at it for a second, then slid it in her back pocket. After smiling at me, she walked away, and I got the best view in the place. I watched her until she met her screaming friends. I slightly rolled my eyes and turned back to guzzle the rest of my drink. She seemed way more mature than the women she kept company with. Leaving a tip for the bartender, I stood from my stool. Giving her another once over, I left. Hopefully she called, but if not, it would be her loss.

Once I got back to my room, I called my mother. She constantly worried about me. After spending three years in prison when I was in my thirties, she's been insistent on me calling her every day. Even though I was no longer into the activities that landed me there, she still didn't quite trust that I would make the right decisions. I ran the streets for almost twenty years and was good about hiding my money. So, when I got out, it was all waiting for me.

After working my ass off and getting a few influential people in Houston to roll with me, I was able to open my first Smoothie King with their backing. It was a legit way for me to remain under the radar with my monetary dealings. I now had twenty stores in the state and was looking into expanding to southern Louisiana. After dialing her number, I sat on the couch in my suite and put my feet up on the coffee table. "Hey, Cole. You had a long day, baby?"

"Yes ma'am, but everything's good. How are you?"

"I'm good. I went to the Nifty at Fifty place and exercised. Then I went to the wellness center for water aerobics."

"That's good, Mama. Did the plumber come and repair the busted pipe for you?"

"He sure did. Thank you, Cole, for taking care of things for me."

"Anything for you, Ma. What good would it be for me to have millions and not have a beautiful mother to spend it on?"

I smiled at the thought of how she'd always been there. Sending her last to put on my books when I was locked up for possession with the intent to distribute was something I would never forget. I couldn't risk telling her where my money was because she would've needed help to get to where it was. I didn't trust anybody past her at the time. I hated that I'd put my sixty-year-old mother in that position. She was almost eighty now, and my older sister wasn't shit. So, my mama's health and well-being all depended on me providing for her. I didn't have a problem with that, though. While she had a social security check coming in, it didn't provide much. I didn't know who the government thought could live on five hundred dollars a month.

She chuckled at my statement, then said, "Well, since you put it that way, I'd have to say that you would be rich and miserable."

I smiled. She was my everything. Knowing that the stress she endured when I was locked up nearly gave her a heart attack was motivation enough to make sure she was always good, although she only accepted the help when it was something dealing with repairs or it was a gift. "I'll be home to visit in a couple of weeks. I wish you would just move to Houston."

"Oh no. That's too fast for me. I wanna do my own thing, baby. I can drive and shop for myself."

"I know. But I would be able to see you more if you were here. Port Arthur ain't got nothing for me, but trouble."

"But you're a changed man. You've been out of that mess for over fifteen years now."

That was true. I was a fifty-one-year-old man, still living in fear of what could happen if I stayed in Port Arthur too long. I had been on the streets since I was fourteen years old, taking care of responsibilities that weren't mine. When I got busted, I'd been doing that shit for almost twenty years. It was practically apart of who I was. Changing the subject, I said, "Get your swimsuit ready, diva. We're going to the Bahamas this summer."

"Really? A seventy-eight-year-old woman in a bikini?"

I laughed. "Now, nobody said nothing about a bikini, Ma."

She laughed as well, then got quiet. When I noticed it was

almost nine, I knew I had kept her up past her bedtime. "Get some rest, Ma, and I'll call you tomorrow. I love you."

"I love you, too, Colson. Have fun in Galveston."

"I'll try to squeeze some fun in."

She chuckled. "Goodnight."

"Night, Ma."

Everything I'd accomplished was worth it when I talked to my mama. Had I not been adamant about succeeding and pushing through the rejection letters and flat out no's to my face, she would be dead by now. Stress was eating her alive. After ending the call with her, I started the shower. I felt weird not working out today, but I'd handle that tomorrow before I went to the beach to chill out. I again thought about Sky and how beautiful she was. I probably didn't have any business with a woman over twenty years my junior. I was pretty sure she was still in her twenties. She didn't seem to have a problem in that area since she came to talk to me, though.

I kept up with my physique and made sure I was always groomed to perfection, but for some reason, I hadn't met that woman that could hold my attention for longer than a fuck. After that, it went downhill. Maybe because we hopped in bed too soon, but hey, I wasn't turning down worthwhile advances. After getting in the shower, I washed my body and my hands of anything happening with Sky.

# S ky

"HE IS SO FUCKING SEXY! YOU BETTER CALL THAT MAN."

I side-eyed my friend, Nikki, and continued getting my pajamas from the drawer to take a shower. "In case you haven't noticed, it's one a.m., and Colson didn't seem to be on vacation. Judging by his attire, he had some sort of job he'd been to. I am *not* calling that man at one in the morning. Maybe I'll call later this evening."

"Maybe? Bitch, you gotta be stupid."

"That man has to be at least fifteen years older than me. While he *is* gorgeous, I don't know how that would work out. Now please drop it."

"One day, you gon' learn to take risks. That's why you damn near thirty with no prospects in sight. If the triflin' teenagers at school hit on you, imagine what an older man thinks of all those curves. Girl, you fine as hell and I wish I had body like you. I'd flaunt that shit everywhere."

"And that's why God saw fit to not give you curves."

"That's okay. I flaunt my slender frame anyway. I'm still fine without the tits and ass."

I rolled my eyes and went to the bathroom. As I stood looking at myself in the mirror, I knew Nikki was right. I was way too picky and could possibly miss out on the man I was supposed to be with. As I looked over my curves, I smiled. When I unleashed this waist trainer, I huffed loudly. "You need to quit wearing that shit so you can breathe!"

"Shut up, Nikki!"

Out of everyone that came on the girls' trip, I didn't know why I had to room with Nikki's crazy ass. Yeah, I did. She was my best friend. I chuckled before I got in the shower. The waist trainer made my clothes fit better, and I liked my waistline to look snatched. So... there. I wore them. My brother used to always say that I needed to be happy with how God made me, but God didn't do this to my body. Shit, I did. All that late night eating I was doing and stressing over tests caused me to gain weight. I'd gotten some of it off and I was happy with the thickness I had going on. It was beautiful on me, but I wanted curves. I didn't want my stomach to stick out as much as my boobs and ass did.

I wasn't downing myself or anyone else. There was nothing wrong with me wanting *my* body to look a certain way. I knew Nikki wasn't saying all of that, but people got on my nerves with their fucking opinions about what I should and shouldn't do with my body and how I should just be happy with the way I was. Most of the ones that were saying that wore false lashes, weaves, and makeup... all things that altered their appearance.

After getting out of the shower, I went back in the room, and surprisingly, I wasn't sleepy yet. Nikki was sprawled out across her bed, snoring. We'd all gotten tipsy, but her even more than me. We were high school teachers in Beaumont and rarely had time where we could let our hair down without someone seeing us and criticizing everything we did. Although Galveston wasn't that far away, it was far enough to have a good time without fear of risking our jobs. It was ridiculous how they expected teachers to be like preachers. I taught math. What in the hell does that have to do with whether I go out and have drinks?

I pulled a stack of papers out of my bag. I'd given a test the Thursday before spring break and I hadn't felt like grading them. All five classes that I taught had at least twenty-five kids in them, so that made quite a few papers to grade. As I seemed to go on autopilot, I thought about Colson. He was so fine. He had to be around forty-five or so. It wasn't like I still had someone to get feedback from. My mama had died from a massive heart attack a couple of years ago, and my dad died of a stroke almost twenty years ago.

I think my mama stressed herself to death. She missed my daddy so much, she literally made herself sick. They'd been married for nearly twenty-five years when he died. So, my brother, Weslan, took on the responsibility of helping Mama take care of me and thought it was his job to boss me around. He got on my damn nerves. I could see him in my head giving Colson the third degree if they ever met. *Why was I thinking about this if I haven't even called the man?* Shaking my head, I focused on my grading. I'd given credit for a couple of problems that weren't correct.

❦

"BITCH, WAKE UP! I KNOW LIKE HELL YOU WEREN'T GRADING papers!"

My eyes opened slowly. Papers were all over my bed and my pen was still in my hand. There was a red line going across the test that was in my lap. *Shit.* I'd fallen asleep. "I couldn't sleep, so I did something constructive."

"I can't believe you even brought the shit out here. We are here to forget about home life for once and have fun! Now get up so we can get some breakfast. We gotta hit the beach today and see what we can see."

I rolled my eyes and organized my papers. I'd gotten two classes graded and was on the third one when I fell asleep. As I peeled myself from the bed, I groaned. My bones were stiff, and I could use one of those massages the hotel offered. I stretched and heard my bones cracking. Stress was something else. The stress of trying to be an amazing teacher, one that the students loved and the administrators praised was challenging, because those two things were hard to do simultaneously. While I was tough and hard on my students, I wanted them to feel like I would do everything I could to help them succeed, regardless of some of their attitudes.

Standing in the mirror, I turned to the side, assessing my figure. That waist trainer was working. Before long, I wouldn't have to wear it as often. After handling my hygiene, I put on my long terrycloth housecoat so we could hurry and get breakfast. Nikki looked at me and rolled her eyes. "Could you look any more homely?"

"Shut up and come on."

When we got to the lobby, there wasn't much food left. They would stop serving breakfast in the next ten minutes. It was almost ten. When we sat, I saw him. *Colson.* Good Lord, the man was fine. He had on a fucking suit. That let me know he didn't live here, either. I wondered where he'd traveled from. He was obviously here on business. *Shit!* He couldn't see me looking this way. "What the fuck wrong wit'chu, Sky?"

She followed my line of vision and smiled. When she stood from her seat, I could've knocked her ass out. The moment she did, his gaze fell on us. He kept walking, then suddenly stopped and looked back at us. Nikki had walked her ass back to get the last couple of pancakes. I swallowed hard, and as badly as I wanted to look away, I couldn't. Colson walked to my table and I could've dived under it. "Hello, Sky. How are you this morning?"

"I'm great. How are you?"

"I'm good. Well, I'm on my way out. I just wanted to speak."

I nodded as he smiled. "Well, have a good day," I said softly.

"You too, beautiful."

He smiled again and walked away. I couldn't stop looking. I wanted to run after his ass in this old maid robe. "That's what yo' ass get. Coming down here looking like that. Fortunately for you, he thinks you're still cute. I can't figure out how, though."

"Shut up, bitch."

She opened her mouth and held her hand to her chest like she was in shock. I rarely used the word bitch. While I knew it was habit for her to say that to women close to her, I tried to refrain from it. But I meant it this time. She was being a bitch just now by getting him to notice me looking like a bum. I rolled my eyes at her and finished off my breakfast so I could put on my fabulous swimsuit and sit under my umbrella and read. But it was good to know that we were staying in the same hotel. I'd make sure he didn't catch me slipping again.

Once we were done eating, we headed back upstairs to get ready for a day of fun and relaxation. I put on my high-waist bikini bottoms and turned to the side in the mirror to see how it made my ass look. I didn't like wearing anything that made my ass look flat. However, it had it sitting up a little higher. I could deal with that. After putting on my top, I looked in the mirror once again. Wearing a bikini was new for me, but the way this one was made, only a sliver of skin in my mid-area was exposed.

Wearing anything showing my legs used to be out of the question. My birthmark was on the outer part of my right leg. As a kid, I used to get teased about it. It looked like liver spots or liver splashes, like my mama used to call it, from my thigh to my calf. So, as soon as I could pick out my own clothes, I chose to cover it up. It wasn't until my college years that I chose to expose it again. I'd found a cute dress that stopped a little above my knee, and I refused to pass it up. It fit me so well. When I finally wore it, no one said a thing about my leg, and at that moment, I felt like whoever had something to say could kiss my entire ass.

From that moment, I became more confident and didn't allow what anyone else said about me to get me down. I knew who I was and what I believed in, and nobody in hell would ever be able to make me feel uncomfortable in my own skin again. Everybody had an opinion, but when it concerned me and my appearance, they could keep their comments to themselves. Unless... "Well, damn. Stunt on 'em, sis!"

Unless they were complimenting me, of course. I smiled and shook my head slowly at Nikki's theatrics. "Thank you, girl."

"What are you wearing over it?"

I showed her the over-sized brown and golden weaved dress that hung off the shoulder. We planned to walk along the seawall and go to different shops in the area. I couldn't be walking around everywhere with my ass hanging out. "Well, hopefully you'll get to see that sexy zaddy later."

I rolled my eyes. "I'm still mad at'chu for that stunt you pulled earlier."

"Whatever," she said as she waved her hand and started the shower.

I began applying my makeup and getting my hair together. Looking flawless made me feel amazing on the inside. It put a lil pep in my step. Dressing up always did that for me. I always felt good about myself, but something about dressing up and having my hair done made me feel even more amazing. When I was done, I got my floppy tan hat and my tan bag for my sunscreen, my mist fan, a book, and scrunchies to pull my hair back. I also snuck my work in the bag, too. Just in case they left me alone on the beach.

Nikki, and our other three acquaintances, Karma, Niecy, and Alex, were all single and relished in the moment. They went looking for action, whereas I let the action find me. Colson had found me. I couldn't stop thinking about him. While he was dressed nicely, I could clearly see the neck tattoo. If he had a tattoo on his neck, I was almost sure he had more. There was something rugged about him. His eyes were mesmerizing. They were low and sexy. That golden colored skin, bald head, and muscular build was sexy as hell. And his smile... dear God. Sun rays surrounded his ass whenever he flashed those pearly whites. He had an air of confidence that just pulled me in.

His salt and pepper beard was what first caught my attention. Beards were my weakness on the right man. Colson's looks were everything. It was like God personally came from heaven and sculpted this man... taking his time to breathe on every inch of his flesh. As I sat on the bed, waiting for Nikki, I pulled the card from my purse. What was I afraid of? His age? That he would take me and did as he pleased? I bit my bottom lip, then grabbed my phone and texted him. *Hi Colson. This is Sky. According to how you were dressed this morning, you're probably busy, but I wanted you to have my phone number.*

My thumb hovered over the send button as I second guessed myself. Before I could think any further, I hit send. My entire body trembled as I waited to see if I would get a response. He was obviously heading out to handle business. It was only noon. When my phone chimed, I nearly jumped out of my skin. Seeing the blue bubbles let me know that he had an iPhone as well. *Well, hello beautiful. I was hoping you'd get in touch. I'm just wrapping up business for the day. What's on your agenda?*

Carefully thinking about how I would word my response to let him know he could pop up on me, I said, *I'm going shopping in a little bit, but I'll be at the beach later. Hopefully relaxing.*

Within a few seconds, he responded. *I would love to spend time getting to know you. I don't have any significant plans. I do plan to go to the beach later as well. So, call me if you have time.*

I smiled at the phone like he was standing in front of me. I was so engrossed, I didn't see Nikki standing in front of me. "What got'chu cheesing and shit?"

I showed her my phone and her mouth opened. "Oh shit! You actually contacted him. I'm proud of you girl!"

Rolling my eyes, I stood from the bed and grabbed my things so we could get our day started. "You know Karma ain't ready, right?"

"What else is new? I'm not about to waste half the day sitting in a hotel, waiting on her slow ass."

"Touché, bitch."

With that, we walked out and headed to my car. As we got to my Kia, what I saw took my breath away. Colson had just arrived back at the hotel. He stepped out of his Escalade and headed towards the hotel entrance. His tie and the top button on his shirt were undone, and he had a frown on his face. Those eyes had lowered to slits, causing me to flood my bikini bottoms. Watching his strides had me licking my lips. I would see him later... no doubt about that shit.

# C olson

I WAS SO FUCKING ANGRY I ALMOST SHUT THE STORE DOWN for the day. When I got to my Smoothie King on Seawall Blvd, I could have shit a brick. They weren't open for business yet. It was almost ten-thirty when I'd gotten there, and they were supposed to open at ten. The assistant manager came running around the corner all flustered, apologizing and telling me that the two people opening both called in. When I asked to see her schedule, she turned red as shit. She was supposed to open along with another person.

It was spring break. I was sure we lost quite a bit of business. Immediately, I called the head store manager, and upon his arrival, I proceeded to fire the other manager and the employee that didn't show up. I told them I would be back later, and this store had better been functioning properly or I'd shut it down until I could replace every last one of them. They'd fucked my mood up, but before I could leave the premises, I got a text message that erased all that shit away.

*Sky.*

She was the most beautiful woman I'd seen in a long ass time. While I didn't really press a woman to spend time with me, I'd pull out all the stops for her. She was younger than me, but so what. I could see her marrying me and having my babies, and I didn't even know her yet. If I had my way, that would soon change. I could tell she had morals and was somewhat reserved when it came to approaching men. That meant that even when she was supposed to be letting her hair down, she remained a lady. The ultimate turn-on.

As I laid across the bed in my suite, I thought of ways to get decent employees at that location. I already paid above minimum wage to all my employees and offered insurance to the full-time employees. I would have to offer something more appealing to get quality workers. Rubbing my hands down my face, I decided to get up and go work out. It cleared my mind and helped me think more clearly. Working out wasn't the only thing that did the trick, but I hadn't been with a woman in months. As much as I flirted, one would think that I'd been with different women every chance I got. Not so.

I liked to see women blush and feel appreciated. My words may be the only compliment they'd gotten that day. To see their smiles brightened my day as well. It helped that I was easy on the eyes. It made them more receptive of my compliments. So, yeah, I was that dude that said 'hey beautiful' to almost every woman I came in contact with. Before I could get out the door, my phone rang. I immediately answered the 409 area code, because that could be someone here in Galveston or my mama. Port Arthur, along with Beaumont and the surrounding areas, all had a 409 area code. Mama was known for losing her phone. "Hello?"

"Cole! What'chu doing?"

I immediately rolled my eyes and pulled the phone from my ear, mouthing, *fuck!* "I'm out of town, about to check on one of my stores. What's the deal, Val?"

Val was my sister and she sounded high as a fucking kite. "I need thirty dollars. You think you can send it through MoneyGram or some shit like that?"

"What'chu need money for, Val? I thought you worked just like everybody else."

"Just say you don't wanna help me, Colson! Don't be judging me! You gon' help me or not?"

"I'll help you get clean, all on my dime. But I'm not gon' fund yo' habit."

"Says the muthafucka that used to sell the shit to all of the Golden Triangle. I hate you!"

"Val! You know I love you. I just hate to see you all strung out and shit. That life is behind me and I want it to be behind you, too."

"Fuck you!"

She ended the call and now, I needed that workout more than ever. I grabbed my keycard and phone, then headed down. So many things were running through my mind. I was almost sure Val had called Mama. She didn't need to be there to have to put up with Val's foolishness. She only saw her when she needed money. Closing my eyes, I said a brief prayer of protection for my mama, and then went straight to the free weights. After getting a spotter, I worked the fuck out of those weights.

When I went back to my room, I felt better. The shit with my sister had made me forget all about my business. After getting out of the shower, my phone was ringing again. I rolled my eyes because I didn't feel like being bothered with no-got-damn-body. Well... there was one person. I looked at the number and when I saw it wasn't her or my mother, I let it ring. If it was important, they'd leave a message. And sure enough, they did. Something told me not to listen, and I obeyed that voice. I tried to follow my gut quite often. Just like my gut was telling me not to answer the phone that was now ringing again. It was the same number. Closing my eyes, I answered anyway. "Hello?"

"They gon' kill me, Colson! That's what you want? He said he was gon' slice me up!"

"Well, your funeral is paid up, so we good, Val."

"You're a heartless muthafucka! This may be your last time talking to me! You willing to let them kill me over thirty-dollars?"

"Bye, Val. See you at the funeral."

I ended the call before she could respond. Somebody was always trying to kill her. She'd do and say anything to get money. Shaking my head, I put on some swim trunks, then basketball shorts and a t-shirt. I was glad I was relaxed before talking to her. I would have cursed Val out. That workout was all for nothing, though, 'cause I was all worked up again. I grabbed my wallet, keys, and a large towel and headed to one of my favorite places to eat: Cajun Greek. It probably wasn't wise to go get full and then sit out in the heat at the beach. So, I'd eat a little just to quench my hunger pains, and then get a smoothie.

WHEN I GOT TO THE BEACH, I RENTED ONE OF THE UMBRELLA chairs and sat near the water. I should have had our meeting in South Padre Island. Galveston's beach wasn't all that pleasant to look at. Seaweed sometimes covered the shoreline and the water was murky. There didn't seem to be much seaweed today, though. I pushed my air pods in my ears and closed my eyes, enjoying the breeze and the relaxing music of my 90's mix until my phone rang. Opening my eyes, I exhaled loudly when I saw my mother's number. I knew it was about Valencia's ass. "Hey, Ma."

She was sniffing, and that only pissed me off. "Cole. Val said somebody's gonna kill her because she owes them money. I don't know what to do. She's said that before, but I don't want to deny her in case she's telling the truth."

"Mama, Val brings all that shit on herself. When is enough going to be enough?"

"I know, but I wouldn't be able to live with myself if something happened to her."

"Okay, Ma. Do what makes you feel better. I understand."

Suddenly there was a loud banging noise. I already knew Val had made her way to Mama's house. "I'll call you back, Colson."

"Naw, Ma. Don't hang up. I need to hear what's going on."

"O... okay," she stuttered.

I could hear the fear in her voice, and it made me wonder if Val had tried anything before. Sitting up in the chair, I turned sideways and took out my air pods, bringing the phone to my ear. As I listened to Mama head to the door, my eyes landed on the most beautiful woman on the beach. When she pulled her cover-up off, I involuntarily licked my lips. *Damn.* Sky was so damn fine. She sat in a chair and took off her floppy hat as her friend went out to the water. Just that quickly, I'd committed her every curve to memory. I'd recognize that body anywhere.

Hearing Val's screaming brought my attention back to the call. "Mama, put me on speaker."

When she did, I heard a loud noise. Standing to my feet I said, "What in the fuck was that?"

Mama moaned, and I said, "Val, I'm gon' fuck you up when I get there. I don't know what you did, but you gon' suffer for it."

"It's okay, Colson. I'm okay," Mama said softly.

She was in pain. I heard Val say, "I'm sorry, Mama. Thank you for the money. I gotta go."

"You better not let me find you, Val. That threat on your life is real, 'cause it's coming from me."

"Fuck you, Colson! You ain't perfect!"

The door slammed. I grabbed my towel from the chair and said, "Mama, I'm going checkout. Hopefully, I'll be there in about three hours. You coming back with me to Houston and I don't wanna hear shit about it."

"Okay."

As I ended the call and picked up my air pods, my eyes met Sky's. Fuck! I wanted to spend time with her. Taking a deep breath, I walked over to her. She stood from her seat and sat her book on the chair. I smiled, trying to calm my nerves. Reaching out for her hand, I said, "You look beautiful."

"Thank you," she said as she blushed. "Are you leaving?"

"Yeah. I have to make an emergency trip to Port Arthur. I wish I could have had time with you today."

"Are you coming back to Galveston?"

"Probably not. I'm not sure how long I'll be in Port Arthur."

"If you're still there Saturday, call me. I should be home."

"Damn. I don't wanna leave, now." My eyes scanned her body and I could see the goosebumps on her flesh. "If I'm still there, I'll call you, but I'll text you later."

I kissed her hand as she nodded. "You can call or text me anytime. Okay?"

"Okay."

It was like pulling teeth to leave her standing there in the sand. Val was gon' definitely get fucked up. She had successfully ruined the rest of my trip. Although I had Sky's phone number, I wanted to get more familiar with her in person versus by phone. After spring break, she could change her mind about me. My calls could go unanswered. I tried to stomp through the sand like a spoiled kid, but that was damn near impossible. Once her hand slid out of mine, I was immediately angry again. There was no telling what condition my mama was in. Although, she said she was okay, she often tried to protect Val.

When I finally got to the sidewalk, I dusted the sand off my legs and feet, then put my shirt on. Glancing back toward Sky, I saw her still standing in the same spot, watching me. *Shit!* She was making me want to run back to her, scoop her up, and take off with her. I held her gaze for a moment and wished like hell I didn't have to leave. It seemed like she was wishing the same thing. I could see how she had scanned my body when I was walking to her. Forcing myself to get in my truck, I started the engine and drove away.

Getting to my room, I slung clothes in my suitcase. I was hot as fish grease, and I was gonna take it out on Val's ass. Once I'd gotten everything packed and had checked out and loaded my luggage, I received a text message. After I got in the driver's seat, I looked at my phone to see, *I wish you didn't have to leave.*

I smiled slightly, then replied, *Me either. Send me a selfie so I can keep seeing that beautiful face.*

Lifting the camera, I took one and sent it to her before pulling out of the hotel parking lot. We had so much to explore. The physical attraction was there for sure. It took a lot to resist pulling her close to me. Her lips were amazing, and I wanted to kiss them. Her picture came through and damn. The sun was shining on her so perfectly. Those plump red lips were somewhat poked out and her eyes looked to be pleading with me to come back. As I was putting my phone down, another picture came through. She was smiling big. "Damn, Sky," I said aloud.

I continued on to the ferry while my mind was still at the beach, wondering about her likes and dislikes and how I would woo her into my bed and my heart. There was something about her that wouldn't let me rest. It was like I'd never seen a beautiful woman until I saw her in the bar last night. When I got to the line, my phone chimed, alerting me of another text. *Be careful and I hope to talk to you soon.*

She was definitely going to hear from me soon. If she wouldn't have been at the beach enjoying herself, I would call her now. I responded, *I wish I could talk to you now. But I'll text you when I get settled in Port Arthur.*

I pounded my steering wheel as I thought about what I was missing out on.

## ❅ 4 ❅

S ky

"BITCH! WAS THAT HIM?" NIKKI ASKED AS SHE RAN UP TO ME.

"Yes. He was leaving but noticed me over here."

"And I take it you feeling him for real, since yo' ass still standing here, looking in the direction he went."

I rolled my eyes as I looked at his picture in my phone. Colson was a gorgeous man. I could stare at this picture the rest of the day. Shit, I could fall asleep to it. And Lord have mercy, his tattooed body was everything I thought it was. They covered his entire chest, shoulders, and parts of his arms and neck. He looked like an arch angel while the sun shown on him. His age was the only thing that kept bothering me. Well... not bothering me, but made me a little hesitant. But it wouldn't hurt to get to know him. "Can you snap out of it?"

"What are you talking about?"

"I said that those other bitches we came here with are on their way, but that shit don't matter since your brain left with his ass. He fine. I'll give you that shit."

I finally sat back down in my chair, repeatedly glancing at his picture. "Let me see this shit," Nikki said as she snatched my phone from me. "Oh, hell yeah. I see why you can't focus."

She handed the phone back and I snatched it from her hands as she sat next to me. "So are you gonna try to get to know him, or will he just be somebody to play with?"

"You saw his picture and you saw him in person. Why would I only want to play with him, Nikki?"

"Bitch, don't get salty with me. If you remember, you were hesitant about his age. So, if you think he's too much older than you, then you would fuck him and move on. That's all I'm saying."

"Yeah, sorry," I conceded. "Something about him is making me lose my damn mind. I can't stop thinking about him nor do I want to. He's so smooth, but I can sense something rough about him. He's like the perfect mix. I don't know what it is actually, but I want to find out."

I looked over at Nikki and she was smiling. "Well, call him. Where did he go?"

"He's from Port Arthur and he needed to go there for some reason or another."

"Well, shit! Does he still live there?"

"No. He lives in Houston."

"Oh okay. Well call him. I got some action over here that I need to tend to," she said while watching a couple of guys throw a football.

I slowly shook my head as I watched her strut her narrow ass into the water right next to them. She got their attention, too. Men were so gullible at times. As I clenched my phone, I warred within myself on whether I should call. He said I could call anytime and that he wished he could talk now through text, but I didn't wanna seem too thirsty. Looking down at my phone at his picture, I made a decision. *Fuck it.* I called him. "Hello?"

"Hi, Colson."

"Hey. I wasn't expecting you to call so soon, but I'm not upset. That's for sure."

I chuckled and said, "I... umm... I'm excited to get to know you."

"Is that right? I feel the same way about you."

I took a deep breath and smiled. His baritone voice was causing a stirring below that I couldn't shake. "Yeah," I said softly. Taking another deep breath to calm my racing heart, I asked, "So, what's your last name? What do you do?"

"My full name is Colson Jermaine Crook. I own quite a few Smoothie Kings throughout Texas and two furniture stores, one in Houston and another in Dallas. What about you? What's your last name and what do you do?"

"That's impressive. Since you gave me your full name, I suppose I'll give you mine. It's Sky Sade Agnes Jones. Agnes was my grandmother. She died the same day my mother gave birth to me. I'm a high school math teacher."

"I could tell you were smart. And I like your name. You'll always carry a piece of your grandmother, although you never got to know her. That's cool. What type of math teacher are you?"

"Statistics and Pre-Calculus."

"Damn. I might need to hire you to run some numbers for me."

I giggled, then addressed my main concern. "If I can ask, how old are you, Colson?"

"Fifty-one. Is that a problem? I hope not."

My heart sank a little. He was older than I thought. "I don't know. I'm only twenty-nine. I've never tried to pursue anything with someone more than a few years older than me."

"Well, let me hit'chu with the pros and cons right quick. Pros numbers one through four. I done lived life, made mistakes, recovered from them, and know exactly what I want out of life. Pro number five. I'm established. You ain't gotta wait for me to fulfill my potential and be disappointed when I don't. Pro number six. I'm in excellent shape, and if it wasn't for this salt and pepper beard, you wouldn't know I was over forty, let alone fifty-one. Pro number seven. I know how to treat a woman. I've lived long enough to know some of the general things that women love and I'm patient enough to learn the personal things *you* love."

Shit. Colson had me stewing in my juices. He stopped talking. I waited for him to continue, but when he didn't, I asked, "And the cons?"

"Oh. Did I say cons? Ain't none."

I laughed as he chuckled. "I suppose you're right. But I guess I should warn you that I have an overprotective big brother who thinks he can still tell me what to do."

"That's okay. I have experience dealing with big brothers, too. What about your parents? Will this be an issue for them?"

"No. Both my parents are deceased."

"Ahh. I see why he's that way, then."

"Yeah. My dad died about twenty years ago and my mom a couple of years ago."

"I'm sorry to hear that. My mama is still living, and that's actually who I'm going to Port Arthur to check on. I have an older sister, and I don't know who my sperm donor is. I mean... I know *who* he is, but I've never met him."

"Oh. That's sad."

"Yeah, but I'm good with it. How long you been teaching?"

"Almost eight years now."

"Wow. That's amazing. I've been running my businesses for a total of about fifteen years."

"That's great. I love Smoothie King."

"What's your favorite?"

"Well, I can't say that I've tried enough to have a favorite, but I always get the Caribbean Way."

"Oh, that's a good one. I like it, too."

We were quiet for a moment. I could tell he'd started driving, so he was probably waiting in line at the ferry. "So, are you gonna try to come back after you check on your mom?"

"Yeah. I'm gonna try. I wanna spend time with you... get to know your mannerisms and as much as I can about you. I really prefer talking in person. It's easier to read between the lines. You know the body says a lot of things that our mouths refuse to say, especially the eyes."

"That's what I hear. So, you gon' try to analyze me, Colson?"

"I'm not gonna try, baby girl. I will. Every inch of you."

The way my body heated up was unreal. It was already hot outside, but I felt my temperature skyrocket. "See how quiet you are, Sky Sade Agnes Jones? I bet your eyes are expressive as hell right now."

"That's probably true," I said a little softer than I planned to.

I was fidgeting like crazy. The way he said my name had my bikini bottoms wet and I hadn't gotten in the water. He chuckled, then said, "I wish I could've seen your face. I bet your lips parted and everything."

"You think you know me already, huh?"

He was right on the money, though. "Sky! Bring yo' ass to the water!"

I waved Nikki off as Colson said, "Go hang with your friends. We can talk later... all night if you want, wit' yo sexy ass."

*Stop it!* My clit was pulsating, begging to be sucked on. Colson was turning me on so damn much. The way he could go from sounding all proper and shit to sounding like the neighborhood dope boy had me beyond intrigued. "Colson, I wanna talk to you, if that's okay. They can go to hell."

He chuckled. "It's beyond okay, baby. So, check this out. When I get back to Galveston, I want you to meet me in the same spot on the beach and we can have a do over. You so attractive, my mama gon' have to leave the land of the trill so I can get back to you."

I laughed at his imitation of Pimp C. "Did you know UGK?"

"Naw. I'm a little older than them, but I saw them around."

"Oh okay. That's cool. What type of things do you like to do in your spare time?"

"I work out, go to the movies, and I like to bowl."

"Are you any good at bowling? I've been wanting someone to give me pointers."

"Naw. I suck. I need pointers myself."

I fell out laughing and so did he. I was enjoying his conversation so much until my friends were all staring at me because I'd been on the phone so long. They were definitely talking about me, but they could go to hell. Colson had my undivided attention until he got to Port Arthur or until he needed to end the call. I haven't talked to a man that kept my attention this way in at least a year, and they weren't going to ruin the amazing time I was having with him, especially since Nikki's ass was the one who'd pumped me up to call him.

Although he was much older than me, the conversation flowed smoothly and didn't seem to be lacking a thing. I'd laughed, felt compassionate, and felt turned on. We'd only been on the phone for about forty minutes. So for me to have felt all those emotions already was amazing and unlike any conversation I've ever had with a man before. I crossed my legs in my chair as I heard his engine start. "Have you finally gotten across?"

"Yeah, we're about to drive off the boat now. You know what?"

"What?"

"Your conversation has been really easy. It feels like I've known you for years."

"I was just thinking the same thing. It's flowed really easy. So tell me, what type of music do you like?"

"I can listen to almost anything, but I prefer rap, R&B, and jazz."

"Wow! Really? Who are some of your favorite artists?"

"I like Rachel Ferrell, Robert Glasper, J. Cole, Tank, Dave

East… I can go on and on, but those were the ones just off the top of my head. What about you?"

"We really have a lot in common. I love all of those artists you just named. Add in Lalah Hathaway, Jhene Aiko, and a few popular 90's artists, and we're the same person."

"Well, you must be the female version of me. I like those as well. You're right. We have a lot in common."

I was cheesing so big. Calling Colson was definitely the right decision and I couldn't get enough of his conversation. Hopefully, he'd make it back to me like he said he would.

## 5

C olson

"MAMA! YOU CAN'T BE SERIOUS. THAT BITCH HIT YOU IN THE face! Look at your eye!" I yelled, holding her still in front of the mirror, forcing her to look at herself. "So if I gotta carry yo' ass out of here, that's what's gon' happen until I can find Val's triflin' ass!"

"Cole! I'm not leaving my house! Val is sick! The person she is right now is not the Val I raised!"

"She's not a young woman anymore. Val is damn near fifty-five. You have to let go before she accidentally kills you one day."

I couldn't believe I was sitting here, explaining to my mother why she had to let Val go. Her eye wasn't terribly blackened, but I could tell that there was a bruise there. I couldn't believe Val had hit her... and in the face. Mama had told me of a couple of times that Val had hit her before, but it was never in the face. I refused to deal with this shit. I began packing Mama's things as I made a call to one of my old connects. He happened to still be on the streets, making people's lives hell, but I needed him to find Val. "What's up, Cole?"

"I need you to find Val's ass and hold her for me."

"Oh, that bitch right here, high as hell. Easy find."

"Yo, hitta. That's still my sister. I'm the only one that's gon' call her a bitch."

"You right. My bad, but I got her."

"A'ight. I'll be there in a lil bit."

After I finished packing Mama's things, I took her keys and put them in my pocket. "Don't leave. I'll be right back."

She sighed heavily as I left. Just because I was no longer in the streets, I was still respected. I wreaked havoc in Port Arthur. That was one of the main reasons I had to get out of here. People never let you forget your past, and that wasn't gonna work if I was trying to move forward in a more positive light. Tonight, though, I was on something totally different. Val was going to rehab by any means necessary. If I had to knock her ass out for her to cooperate, that was what was going to happen.

When I got there, I gave the lil nigga at the door a head nod. He'd seen me around before, chasing down Val's ass. When I walked in, another nigga held a gun up at me to stop. He was about to frisk me when Jeremy said, "Naw, fam. He good. He always packing, but he good people."

I gave him a head nod as I looked at Val sitting right next to him with that fucking pipe between her lips. I snatched it right from her and stomped that shit. She nearly lost her fucking mind. She lunged at me, and I caught her frail ass and threw her back to the couch while Jeremy tried not to laugh. Ain't shit was funny about this. I snatched her ass up and literally drug her out the house as she screamed obscenities. "Shut the fuck up, Val! I oughta punch you in yo' shit like you did Mama."

"I didn't punch Mama!" she screamed.

I opened my truck and threw her in the passenger seat, then

grabbed her by her neck. "You get out this truck, I'm gon' shoot yo' ass. And I'm not playing wit'cho crackhead ass."

I could feel my lip twitching. That wasn't a good sign. I was beyond angry and liable to make good on the threat I'd just made. I slowly released her neck as she stared at me wide-eyed. Strapping her seatbelt, I could see her facial expression in my peripheral. If she could get away with killing me, she would have done it right then. I closed her door and watched her as I made my way to the driver side. When I got in, she looked over at me and said, "I hate you."

"Good."

I drove until we got to Gulf Coast Rehabilitation Center. She unstrapped her seatbelt quick as hell. I pulled my gun on her and she stopped dead in her tracks. "I'm not playing wit'cho ass, Val. Pick yo' poison. Either way, crack ain't gon' be on the menu. Emergency room or rehab?"

She sat back in the seat as I got out of the driver seat and walked around the vehicle. When I opened her door, I yanked her out by her arm. "You better be glad I ain't fucked yo' ass up."

She rolled her eyes. Val was so fucking high, it was ridiculous. I was surprised she hadn't passed out by now. "You go in here acting any kind of way about being here, I'm gon' make you regret every pull you took off that fucking pipe. I'm sick of dealing wit'cho shit. This is my last attempt to help you get yo' ass right. I'm moving Mama out of here, so you ain't gon' have no fucking body but me. So, fuck up this time and you on yo' own."

After filling out all kinds of paperwork, I realized Val had fallen asleep sitting next to me. Shaking my head slowly, it was probably a good thing she was high. Had she not been, she would have been tryna climb these walls like a fucking cat. They scooped her ass up and brought her to the back. I dropped a bag of toiletries I'd picked up before going get her ass and a couple of pajama sets from the dollar store. I ain't have time for shit else, and the dollar store was on my way. "So, she won't be able to check herself out, right?"

"Right. Unless she somehow sneaks out. That's happened before."

"A'ight. Just make sure y'all watch her as closely as you watching me right now."

I knew she liked what she saw, but it wasn't shit for me in P.A.T. I left for a reason, and I wasn't trying to form a relationship with nobody out here. That only brought my thoughts back to Sky. The woman at the desk gave me a frown, but her eyes didn't leave me. I walked out of that place and headed back to my mama. Did I actually believe that Val was gon' stay at the rehab? Hell, naw. But I knew it would buy me some time to get Mama moved. She was probably gon' be miserable in Houston, but I couldn't risk Val really hurting her or worse.

When I got back to her house, she was sitting in the same spot, crying. I couldn't let her tears sway me. I loaded her luggage in my truck. "Come on, Ma. Stop crying. We gon' go to Galveston in the morning and I'll treat you to a spa day while I get some stuff setup for you in Houston. You'll have your own driver to take you wherever you wanna go, except Port Arthur. We gon' figure this out."

She rolled her eyes and I did the same. She was so fucking stubborn when it came to Val. If I felt like Val was harmless, I'd leave her in this shithole she called home. With as much money as I had given her over the years, she didn't want to leave or at least upgrade this piece of shit. The only thing she'd allowed me to do was normal maintenance, seal in the holes and replace the roof. The appliances were all old as fuck, too. I'd sent all new ones: a stove, fridge, dishwasher, and microwave. She sent all that shit back to the store. When they called me and said they were sorry I wasn't happy with the purchases and would be refunding my credit card, I nearly came unglued.

I really wanted to head back to Galveston, but something about being on the ferry at night bothered the hell out of me. All that water and not being able to see shit gave me chills. Going to my old room, I sat on the hard ass bed and pulled out my cell phone. I sent

Sky Sade Agnes Jones a text message. I chuckled at the recollection of how she said Agnes. *Hey, Ms. Jones. I've gotten things situated. You busy?*

I stood and took off my shirt and pants, leaving my mama's keys in them and laid back in the bed just as Sky texted back. *Hey, Mr. Crook. I'm at a bar... bored out my mind.*

I chuckled at her eyeroll emoji. She wasn't the going out type unless she had a few drinks in her. Even then she was a little uncomfortable. I noticed that last night. *I wish I was there to keep you company. Try to have a good time and I'll see you on the beach tomorrow, same spot.*

I had to hold her in my arms or at least hug her. My need for affection had definitely risen after dealing with Val and my mama. I usually smoked a cigar or a blunt, but I refused to buy that shit out here. Niggas were really haters sometimes, especially when they saw where you rose from. I could see one of them selling me that synthetic shit. My phone chimed again, causing me to smile slightly. *Tomorrow? I'm so excited! What time?*

*Is ten too early?*

That was the time I was scheduling Mama for her spa day. I wanted to see Sky as soon as I could, so I could spend time with her while Mama was occupied. *No, it's not too early. See you then.*

I plugged my phone to my charger and set my alarm for five. We were leaving as early as possible. I hated this place.

WE'D GOTTEN SETTLED IN MY ROOM AND I'D WALKED MY mama downstairs to her appointment. She hadn't said a word to me since last night. Velma was so damned stubborn. I had my moments, but shit. Her face was in the damn dictionary next to the word. Even after I kissed her cheek and said that I would be back at two, she still refused to say a word. That was okay, though, because nothing could bring me down today. I was going to meet that beautiful sunflower in the sand. When I got in my SUV, she was texting. *Good morning. I'm here.*

I smiled. My hotel was only down the street, so I didn't text back. I could see her from my spot on the seawall. She looked so beautiful. She'd worn another bikini. All that thickness oozing out of that shit was gon' be distracting as hell. I got out of the truck, grabbing my towel and my shades, then made my way to her. Her sheer cover-up was blowing in the breeze as I tilted my head to admire her figure. *Damn.*

When I got closer to her, she turned to see me approaching her and smiled brightly. "Hey. I thought you were gonna stand me up."

"Why would you think that, beautiful?" I asked as I grabbed her hand and kissed it.

"I guess you have me spoiled already with immediate responses when I text."

"Well, I was right down the street. I'm here, too."

She laughed, and said, "Give me hug."

"Shit, gladly."

When I pulled her in my arms, I didn't wanna let her go. She was so damn soft and her nails on my back were sending my mind places it shouldn't have been just yet. As she pulled away, I grabbed her hand and led her out to the water. She hesitated some, so I turned around to see her taking her cover-up off. I released her hand to watch her in all her glory. When she turned, I noticed the darker melanin marks on her leg. Probably her birthmark. She turned back to me and smiled, then reached out for my hand. As we walked to the water, I pulled her closer to me, feeling the tremble surge through her. Turning to face her, I said, "I finally get to be in your presence again."

"I know. Last night seemed to drag on forever."

I held both her hands in mine as we waded out a little farther. "Do you know how to swim?"

"I do, but I don't."

I frowned slightly until she laughed. "I know how to swim, but I choose not to unless I'm prepared."

"Oh," I chuckled. "I'm not tryna swim in this water. I ain't going out *that* far. I just wanted to know for future purposes, like if we went someplace else with cleaner, nicer beaches."

"Are you asking me to go with you on a future vacation?"

"If we are compatible... as I believe we are," I said, pulling her closer to me. "I think we would enjoy seeing the world together."

She blushed and averted her gaze. Biting her bottom lip, she looked back at me, then lifted her arms, resting them on my shoulders. My hands instinctively went to her waist, pulling her even closer. We stared into one another's eyes, not saying a word. I glanced down at her cleavage. I couldn't help it. It was right there for me to see. A slight smile made its way to her lips and she said, "Let's go sit down."

"A'ight."

Glancing at me again, she led the way to the chairs. I let her walk out of the water first so I could catch a glimpse at all that ass. When she sat, I sat next to her and continued holding her hand as I took my shades off. I turned to look at her and she smiled, then asked, "How did things go last night?"

I rolled my eyes and she said, "Uh oh."

"Right. My mom is here with me. I have a sister that umm..." I didn't know if I should reveal that or not, but I did anyway. "She's on drugs. She attacked my mama for some money. After all that, she still didn't wanna leave. I had to literally force her to leave the house."

"Oh wow."

"Yeah. But enough of that. What do you plan to do this weekend?"

"Just grade papers and relax until school starts."

"Recoup from the vacay. How did last night go for you?"

"I would have rather talk to you all night."

She leaned into me as I licked my lips. I wanted to kiss her lips so bad. Leaning in closer to her, she closed her eyes as if she was anticipating it. When her lips parted slightly, I went for it. It was soft and I allowed it to linger only for a second or two. After I pulled away, her eyes opened, and she smiled. "Damn. That was amazing, Sky."

"Yes, it was," she purred.

I leaned in again and kissed her lips until I heard someone clearing their throat. "Uh, huzzy! You just gon' leave the room without saying anything?"

Sky rolled her eyes and laughed. "Nikki, really?"

The woman she referred to as Nikki, smiled, then extended her hand to me for a handshake. "I'm Nikki. Thanks for making her step out of her comfort zone."

I smiled slightly. "I'm Colson. Nice to meet you."

It wasn't nice to meet her. She interrupted one of the best moments of my life. Feeling Sky's lips against mine was something I never wanted to do without. As they talked amongst themselves, I took the moment to text my mother. *How's it going?*

Before I could sit the phone down, she responded, *Fine.*

She was still salty, but she could stay that way for all I cared. I wasn't gonna sit and wait for Val to beat the fuck out of her.

## ❧ 6 ❧

S ky

WHILE COLSON WAS ON HIS PHONE, I MOUTHED, *GET THE fuck outta here*. Nikki couldn't take a hint to save her damn life. She kept rambling on and on until I just ignored her ass. Colson seemed to do the same. He grabbed my hand, and asked, "You wanna get something to eat?"

"Oh, yall just gon' straight brush a sister off?"

"I know we just met, but you don't seem to be able to take a hint well."

Nikki's mouth fell open and I laughed loudly. Colson stood from his seat as I said, "Oh, I really like you. Anybody that can have Nikki speechless is number one in my book."

"Bitch..." she mumbled as she walked off with a smirk on her face.

Colson's eyebrows had risen slightly. "Excuse her language."

"Oh, I'm not tripping on her language. It's just; you didn't strike me as the type to let anyone call you that."

"Normally, I don't. She's the only exception."

He smiled slightly and nodded, then grabbed my hand. As we walked through the sand, I couldn't help but fantasize about a future with him. He was such a gentleman and his kisses were sweet like honey. Had Nikki not rudely interrupted us, I would have gone into a diabetic coma. My glucose levels had to be sky high. Colson Jermaine Crook was stealing all my attention and I wasn't mad about it. Who would have ever thought I would be dating a man almost twice my age? But if he was the one, who was I to argue with destiny?

He led me up the stairs to a beautiful, wine-colored Escalade on what had to be twenty-four or twenty-six-inch rims. "Well, damn. I guess the smoothie business is lucrative."

He chuckled as he helped me in the passenger seat. "It's extremely lucrative," he said seductively.

I smiled as he closed the door, then wondered, *what in the hell are you doing in this man's vehicle?* I really didn't know Colson, and here I was leaving with him. He smiled at me, kissed me, and said food. I was totally gone... had to be. Today was the first day we'd spent more than ten minutes around each other, and I was acting like a naïve teenager. When he joined me, he smiled and started the engine. Not taking off immediately, he grabbed my hand. "Thank you for spending time with me. It's been a while since I've had companionship."

I smiled back. He had to be lying with as gorgeous as he was. There was no way he didn't have a woman at his beckoning call somewhere. "So, what do you like to eat?" he asked.

"I'm not too picky. What about you?"

"I love seafood. Is that cool if we eat that?"

"Of course."

He drove away from the curb, merging in with the spring break traffic and parked at a restaurant about a block away on the other side of Seawall Blvd. Had the street not been so busy, we could have walked. When he got out of the vehicle, I took a deep breath. *Relax Sky. Let your hair down and have some fun.* As he opened my door, I smiled brightly at him and he returned the gesture. Colson helped me out of the vehicle, and then slipped his shirt on. I poked my lip out and he chuckled, then grabbed my chin. "What's that face for?"

I slid my hands up his chest underneath his shirt. "You had to cover this perfection."

His face reddened some and I could clearly see his erection as he stared at me. His eyes were speaking to me and they were warning me of how deadly he could be. How he would kill the pussy, damaging every nerve in it. Colson gently tipped my head up and said, "You don't want to wake that up in me... not now."

He was serious as hell as he grabbed me by my waist and roughly pulled me to him. That only turned me on more, and I could feel my nipples harden. Feeling his erection against me made me forget all about seafood, and I wanted to see the food he was wanting to feed me. I pulled on my bottom lip with my teeth as he stared at me with the sexiest frown I had ever seen. Shit, it felt like I was gonna cum on myself. My heart rate had soared, but my breathing was shallow as hell. I didn't know whether I was coming or going. "Now, are we gonna go eat or not?" he asked as if he were insinuating that I had an option.

"If we don't go eat, what else will we do?"

"You sure you wanna find that out? I don't think you ready for that. I'm tryna be a gentleman."

"Well, let's go eat. We can always make time for other things later."

He licked his lips and stepped a little closer to me. "You sure?"

I went on my tip toes and pulled his face to mine, then kissed those amazing lips. My hands traveled to his bald head and he pulled away from me, separating our lips and rested his head against mine. He said in a low voice near my ear, "Damn, girl."

I slowly pulled away from him before I lost all inhibitions and fucked him in his vehicle. It was spring break, and we'd witnessed people fucking all over the damn beach. It was so crowded, but even more so in the evenings. After the first day, we made sure to be far from the beach by three. I'd even run into a few of my students. He closed the door, never taking his eyes off me, and grabbed my hand so we could go inside. *Lord have mercy.* The way he licked his lips had me dying for him to lick between my lips... down south.

When we walked in the restaurant, all eyes were on us. I knew we were a good-looking couple but damn. Then I realized it was because of our attire. Everyone else had actual clothes on. None of the workers seemed bothered by our attire, and Colson seemed to ignore the onlookers. As we sat, the waitress immediately approached us to take our drink orders. Colson reached for my hands. "You okay? You look uncomfortable."

"We just seem to be the center of attention."

"Cause we the finest couple of people this restaurant has ever seen."

I giggled. Colson made me feel so relaxed, and I couldn't help but enjoy his company and forget about everyone else. As I stared at him, our waitress returned with our drinks and took our appetizer order. Soon after she left, a gentleman approached our table. "Colson Crook?"

"Yes."

"I'm Harry Stone. I own a couple of Smoothie Kings in Houston. I thought that was you."

Colson stood and extended his hand to shake Mr. Stone's, then said, "Nice to meet you. This is my lady, Sky Jones."

*His lady, huh?* Wishful thinking. Or maybe not. It was flattering that he was claiming me as his. Mr. Stone nodded at me with a smile as his eyes traveled down my body. I think Colson noticed because a slight frown made its way to his face. Mr. Stone turned his attention back to Colson and said, "I just wanted to introduce myself since we were in the same business. You only have the one on Bissonet, right?"

"No. I have five in Houston, one here in Galveston, and another fourteen throughout the state."

I saw that man's eye twitch, and I couldn't help but smile with pride. They always thought we were inferior. Well his ass got a wakeup call just now. *Jackass.* "Wow. That's impressive. We'll have to get together sometimes. Maybe I can learn something."

Colson nodded, but I knew that type of nod anywhere. It screamed, *fuck you!* When Mr. Stone walked away, Colson turned his attention back to me. "The old me would have fucked his old ass up. Excuse my language."

Well, damn, if the old him wasn't turning me the hell on. "Who was the old you? I think I caught a glimpse just now. He seemed hot headed and dangerous."

"Shit, that ain't the half of it."

He chuckled and I did, too, but mine was more of a nervous chuckle. Who was this man? "So, tell me the half of it."

"Maybe another time, baby girl. Let's just enjoy lunch."

*Hmm.* I guess it was more to it than I imagined. Perusing the menu, I figured out what I wanted to order, then sat it down and stared at him. The frown was still on his face as he looked over the menu. *Damn, he was sexy.* I suppose he felt my gaze on him, because a smirk appeared on his face. Without looking up at me, he said, "You been staring a while. What do you want to ask me?"

"Nothing. I'm just thinking."

"Well, don't think too hard. Who I was then doesn't define who I am now." He looked up at me, and grabbed my hands. "I promise, when the time is right, I'll tell you all about it."

His smile pushed all the suspicions away. I smiled back and said, "Okay."

The waitress took our orders, and just as I was about to ask more about his mother, my phone rang. Glancing at it, I saw my brother's number. Looking at the ceiling, I exhaled loudly. "I'm sorry, Colson. If I don't take this, he'll keep calling until I answer."

He nodded as he watched me answer the phone. "Hello?"

"Sky, where are you?"

"I said hello, Weslan."

"I'm sorry. Hey. Now, where are you?"

"I'm in Galveston."

"Where in Galveston?"

"Why? Last I checked, I was pretty grown."

"Because I just talked to Nikki. She said you went to lunch wit'cho new boo. Who the hell is yo' new boo?"

"I will talk to you later. I'm on a date. It's rude to be on the phone," I said while rolling my eyes.

"A'ight. Call me as soon as you're done."

"Bye Weslan."

I was gon' bitch slap Nikki when I caught up with her ass. Why in the hell would she tell Weslan that shit? She had to have called him, because he had no reason to call her. She was on that bullshit and she was gon' know about that shit as soon as I saw her ass. I shoved my phone back in my purse as the gorgeous man across from me watched in silence. "I'm sorry. That was my nosy-ass brother."

"It's okay. I take it y'all don't get along as well as you would like?"

The thug in him had totally dissipated, and the educated businessman was sitting across from me. "We get along until I'm doing something he doesn't approve of or doesn't know about beforehand. Once that happens, we're like oil and water. He treats me like I'm still a little girl. However, I haven't had a reason to really go against his wishes."

"What if he doesn't approve of us?"

"Then, I guess it's a first time for everything. I'm not going to stop talking to you because he doesn't approve. He can kiss my fat ass."

"And fat it is, baby. Fat as hell."

By his mannerisms, I knew that was a compliment. He licked his lips, then smiled at me as my face heated up. "Why are you blushing?"

"Because it feels amazing to get compliments from a man that I'm actually interested in."

He smiled as the waitress brought back our shrimp bisque and toast. *So mysterious and sexy.* "Well, I'm glad I have your interest. When I first saw you, I knew I wanted to get to know everything about you."

"Mmm. I tried to resist you, but it didn't work out too well."

"Why is that?"

"Because you're so damn sexy. That smile is everything and you know that shit. Those eyes, though. Mm, mm, mm. They could have me in a trance. The way they're shaped... they're just gorgeous."

He smiled at me as he stared in my eyes. "Thank you. I've never met a woman that didn't mind being as straight forward as you while maintaining her class. I appreciate that."

I chuckled. "What do you mean?"

"Your compliments. The women I've met that are as straight forward as you only want one thing."

"How do you know that I don't only want one thing?"

"If that was all you wanted, I would have gotten it by now. I would have gotten it night before last."

"Oh, you smooth with it, huh?"

"Hell yeah. I'm glad you want more, though, because I do, too."

I shied away from his gaze and ate more of the bisque. He was right on the money. I was sick of the scene. I wanted a fine ass man to snatch my ass up and give me the world. It seemed he might be just the man for the job. "So, what are you doing when we leave here?"

"Nothing. Going check on my mama. What about you?"

"I have to talk to Nikki, and then I'd love to spend more time with you."

"That can be arranged, baby."

⚘

"You know I don't really like calling you a bitch, but that was some bullshit you pulled earlier. Why in the fuck would you call Weslan and tell him my business?"

"I said I'm sorry. It's just that you been all wrapped up in him and I wanted some time with you one on one. We rarely get that. These other bitches always around."

"That shit was so childish. Wasn't it yo' ass that said I needed to quit tripping and talk to this man? Now that I am, you tryna sabotage the shit. I don't get that. I'm really feeling him, but I want to get to know him more before Weslan starts asking me a bunch of questions I don't even know the answers to yet."

Nikki sat there looking like a scolded child as I got dressed. I had to get out of this room with her before I knocked that pitiful look off her face. After I slipped on a sundress, I went down to the bar. It was still early, but I needed a damn drink. Nikki had my nerves so bad, only hard liquor would mellow them out... or dick. Dick wasn't a possibility right now, though. Colson was sharing a room with his mother and I was being hot in the bikini bottoms earlier. I could *not* sleep with him this soon. My mama would be turning over in her grave. I wanted his ass, though. If I got drunk enough, I'd fuck him anyway. Mama would just have to be turning.

As I sipped my Long Island Iced Tea, a gentleman sat next to me. "What's a pretty woman like you doing sitting all alone at a bar?"

"She's waiting on her man."

I turned on my stool to see Colson standing directly behind me. He leaned over and kissed my lips as the gentleman stood and left.

46

He sat in his now empty seat with a smirk on his face. I chuckled, then asked, "How dare you run off a prospect?"

"The only thing he was a prospect of was wasting your time. You know I got your mind sewed up. So, why you down here drinking?"

"Nikki pissed me off. Why are you here?"

"My mama pissed me off."

"Well to say the both of us are pissed off, why are we smiling so much?"

"Because we're good for each other and our spirits know it, so it's shining on the outside."

I smiled even bigger, making my eyes look like slits. He slid his finger down my cheek and said, "You're so beautiful."

"You're extremely handsome. I hate that we don't have much time left to spend together."

"Don't worry. I'll be making frequent trips to Beaumont. What school do you teach at?"

"West Brook High School."

"Okay. They played football against one of my friends' school back in the day. You like it?"

"It can be a challenge most days. Kids are less and less disciplined. They installed metal detectors before spring break. That breaks my heart. Beaumont is a small city, and we shouldn't be having these types of problems. But we do. It makes it hard on the teachers. Not only do we have to teach kids that don't wanna learn, but we have to be on guard all the time for if someone has ill intentions. It's exhausting and it takes the pleasure out of it. "

"I hate to hear that."

"Yeah, me, too. I used to think I could make a difference, but I'm not so sure anymore."

Colson grabbed my hand and softly caressed the top of it with his thumb, then ordered me another Long Island Iced Tea and ordered himself a Hennessey. "So, why are you pissed at your mom?"

"Because she isn't speaking to me. She wants to go back to Port Arthur. I'm almost tempted to bring her back. I'm just worried that my sister is going to really hurt her or worse next time. Then I'll feel like I didn't do enough to protect her. On top of that, the rehab center I brought my sister to before coming back here called me. She's in the wind. I don't know how they let her leave. But that's the problem with Port Arthur. Nobody gives a fuck. I'm almost sure Val done made a trip to my mama's house. Had she been there, ain't no telling what would have happened."

"I'm sorry. Well, let's forget about our problems and just enjoy one another's company."

He grabbed my hand. "As soon as you tell me why you're pissed at your friend, we can do just that."

I gave him a tight smile and filled him in on Nikki's shenanigans while he frowned. Just verbalizing that shit sounded shady as hell. It was like as long as I was available to do whatever she wanted to do, I was good as gold. But as soon as I was finally doing something for me, it was a problem. That shit sounded like she never really cared for my happiness at all or respected me. That shit hurt me to my heart, because I always thought Nikki was genuine. Colson hadn't done a thing to prove that it may be a bad decision to spend time with him. So, it wasn't like I was being foolish in that regard.

After I finished talking, Colson took my hand in his again and kissed it. "I'm sorry, baby girl, but it don't seem like she was ever a real friend to you, just somebody to pass time with and gas her up when she needed it."

I hated to agree with him, but her latest shenanigans made it seem that way. She and I would have to have a long ass talk.

## ✤ 7 ✤

C olson

"You know if you actually took the time to enjoy what I was providing for you, you would see that it wasn't so bad. But all you can be is stubborn about shit. I'm getting sick of it."

"You weren't saying all that when I was doing shit for you those years you were locked up, Cole! Now that I'm trying to help Val, it's a problem. That's what the hell I'm angry about! Let me help her like I helped yo' ass!"

I took a step back and stared at her. The very person she was trying to help was trying to harm her. True, she helped me tremendously those years I was locked up, but I wasn't physically attacking her, either. "So, you're telling me I should understand when Val pops you in the face, because you went through that same shit for me? Fine. I'll bring you home. Don't call me when she comes back there acting a fool. She's not in rehab anymore because she snuck

49

out. Val has been on this downward spiral for over ten years. So, if you gon' follow her to hell, that's on you. At some point, you gon' have to let go."

I was sick of this shit. We were supposed to be leaving Galveston to go to my place in Houston, but instead, I was about to drive right back to Port Arthur. I wanted to make sure she was safe, but I was the bad guy in her eyes. That was cool, though. I'd give her what she wanted. Maybe on the way back, I could visit Sky in Beaumont. I had an amazing time with her the other day. We didn't spend much time talking yesterday because she spent it with her girls, and I wanted to show my mama a good time. I'd taken her shopping and to lunch.

As I finished packing my suitcase. My phone rang, breaking me from my thoughts. Grabbing it from the countertop, I answered, "Hello?"

"Hey. We're about to leave and I would love see you before we go."

"I'm on my way down."

I ended the call and grabbed my suitcase, then snatched my mama's suitcase from her hand. I knew I would have to apologize later for that, but she pissed me off. My anger was still consuming me, and I hoped seeing Sky would make it dissipate a little. Leaving my mama in the room, I left out the door and headed down. When I glanced out at the lobby from the glass encased elevator, I saw Sky standing there near the bar waiting on me. It was only ten, but I could use a drink. Once I got off the elevator, I headed to her.

When she looked at me, her face brightened and it made me smile, momentarily forgetting my troubles as I'd hoped. I sat our luggage down and went to her. Grabbing her hand, I brought it to my lips and kissed it, never breaking eye contact with her. "Hey. I see you're heading out, too," she said, glancing at my suitcases.

"Yeah, to Port Arthur."

Her eyes widened. "Why?"

"We got into it this morning, because she was tripping still. So, after that I told her I would bring her back, but not to call me if my sister popped her ass again." I exhaled hard and continued. "I didn't mean that, but I was angry."

Gently pushing her hair from her face, I rested my hand at the back of her neck and pulled her to me. She wrapped her arms around me and said, "I was hoping I would get to feel your embrace."

"You think I can come see you in Beaumont later?"

She lifted her head from my chest and asked, "Really?"

"Yeah. Why would I ask?"

She shook her head like she was trying to rid herself of thoughts and said, "I'm sorry. Of course it's okay. Just call me."

"You okay?"

"Yeah, I'm cool. The past few days have been great talking to you and seeing you."

"It *has* been great, and it won't stop if I can help it. I'm really flexible, so I plan to see you at least twice a week. I hope that's cool with you."

"It's beyond cool with me, baby."

I ran my thumb across her bottom lip as I got lost in her eyes. My mind was miles away until I heard someone clearing their throat. I knew that sound anywhere. I rolled my eyes and turned around to see my mother. Pulling my phone from my pocket, I started the truck and unlocked the doors. "It's open," I said to her, then turned my attention back to Sky.

I could see my mama still standing there in my peripheral, looking at Sky with a shocked look on her face. "Is that your mom?"

"Yeah."

"She's beautiful. Are you going to introduce me?"

"Nope. It has nothing to do with you. I've had it up to here with her shit today," I said, holding my hand above my head, gesturing what 'up to here' meant.

Before I could continue my conversation with Sky, my mother

walked over and held her hand out to Sky. "Hi. I'm Velma, his mother."

"Hi. I'm Sky. Nice to meet you."

I glanced at her, waiting for her to say more, but she didn't. She nodded at Sky, then walked out the door to my truck. Pulling Sky back to me kind of roughly, I quickly let her go. "My bad. I apologize. You're like my little bit of peace and I didn't want you to meet the chaotic piece of my life yet."

"It's okay."

She slid her hands up my chest to my face and pulled it to hers. Kissing my lips slowly and gently, I felt myself totally relax. Sky was my distraction, and I appreciated her for being that for me at this moment. I believed she realized it even before I said it. When she pulled away from me, she said, "I have to go. I can't wait to see you later. Maybe we can meet for dinner."

"Sounds like a plan. You pick the place. I should be there by six."

"Okay. See you soon."

Before she could walk away, I pulled her back to me and pecked her lips again. Grabbing our suitcases, I walked her out the doors and to her car, which happened to be two cars over from mine. After putting the suitcases in my trunk, I walked her over to it. "Please be careful, Sky. Maybe we'll get to talk more as we wait for the ferry."

"Yeah, maybe so. I was trying to avoid the traffic heading out of here by leaving today instead of tomorrow."

"Same here."

She giggled as I opened her car door. Watching her beautiful, thick legs stretch open, I could feel my dick hardening. This would be the first time that I consistently dated a woman in years, but Sky was worth every minute. She was sweet and straight forward. I liked that about her. Although she reneged on sex, I never brought it up again. I knew she didn't really wanna go there with me so soon. She didn't even seem like the type. While she may have been fantasizing about sex with me, actually going there would take some time, and I didn't mind. I'd gladly wait to take my time filling her with joy, literally and figuratively.

Once I closed her door, I watched her drive away. She was gonna be mine, whether she knew it or not. I wouldn't rest until she was. I walked back to my truck and got in as my mama stared at me. "She's beautiful. Is she your girlfriend?"

"No, she's not."

I wasn't trying to engage in conversation with Velma right now. I was trying to remain peaceful by thinking about Sky. Having conversation with Velma would most likely end in disaster. We used to have great conversations, even though she was stubborn as hell then, too. It just seemed to get worse over the years. Before I could get off Seawall Blvd, she asked, "You weren't going to even introduce her to me?"

"No. I wasn't. Mama, please stop acting like we're on good terms right now. While Val is your daughter and my sister, you pretty much compared me to a crack fiend, saying that I was detrimental to your well-being and overall health. I take offense to that, real shit. I've done nothing but try to provide for you and protect you, but I'm the one that gets their hand bit off. I mean, you literally biting the hand that feeds you. But whatever. Sky is my peace right now from this madness between you and Val. She helps me clear my head of the confusion. I didn't want my peace meeting my chaos right now."

She turned and looked out the window, and I let her. Thankfully, she didn't try to say another word and I was grateful. When we got to the line for the ferry, there were only a few cars there waiting, and Sky was in front of me. Although we wouldn't be able to talk out here, we would definitely get to enjoy the boat ride back to the mainland. I couldn't wait to wrap my arms around her waist from behind and enjoy looking out at the water. It would be a peaceful fifteen-minute ride before my drive to the mouth of hell.

As I drove to Cheddars, I was doing my best to put my mind at ease. We'd gotten to Port Arthur at two after stopping for lunch. Mama and I hadn't said a word to one another the whole damn ride back. The music was playing, and my mind was gone fishing. When I'd decided to stop for lunch, she looked over at me and said, *I didn't think you cared whether I ate or not since everything is on your timing*. It took everything in me not to curse my own mama out. I swore she was so got damn overdramatic! She made a big deal out of everything.

After we ate, she tried to pay for her food, and when I wouldn't let her, she still left the money on the table. I snatched it up and shoved it in my pocket. When I caught up with her, she had the nerve to say that since I wanted to tell her not to call me anymore, that she could take care of herself. I had to remind her that it was my fucking money she'd left on the table. So, while I was trying to mellow out so I could leave her in Port Arthur on good terms, that didn't quite work out. Depending on how late it was when I left Sky, I'd go back and apologize. But because of her shenanigans, I was running late.

When I parked in Cheddars' lot, I got out and looked around for Sky at the outdoor patio, but I didn't see her, so I walked inside. The moment I looked over at the bar, I saw her sitting there as the bartender smiled in her face. They looked familiar. Deciding to watch for a moment, he grabbed her hand and kissed it while she laughed, then she waved him off. Making my way over, my slight irritation was probably on my face. She wasn't mine, and I didn't have a right to claim her as such, but I couldn't help but do so anyway. Once I got close, she smiled brightly at me. I leaned over and kissed her puckered lips. "Hey, baby girl."

"Hey. As you can see, it's pretty crowded. I've been waiting for like fifteen minutes already. She told me it would be a forty-minute wait."

"Damn. Can't we just order from the bar?" I asked as I sat next to her.

"Yeah, as long as we're ordering drinks."

She handed the electronic device they'd given her to alert her of when the table was ready to the bartender. He gave us a weird look, and then did as she asked. "You know him?"

"Yeah. He's one of my brother's friends. He's always had a crush on me, but I suppose with you here now, he clearly gets the message that I don't want him."

That was good to know. I could definitely tell that they knew each other. Grabbing her hand, I brought it to my lips and kissed it softly. "So how was the drive back?"

"It was good. I was wishing I could have talked to you on the drive."

"You could have. At least somebody would have been talking to me."

I proceeded to tell her how Velma was acting like a spoiled ass child. I didn't stay on the subject long, though. I was trying to get to know her and get used to being around her. Once we were done with dinner, I walked her out to her car. She leaned against it and I leaned against her. "So, what's up? The night is still early."

Her breathing was shallow as a car sped up right next to us. I frowned as she rolled her eyes. Taking a step back, I got in a defensive stance. "That's my overprotective brother. I'm sure his jealous friend called him."

I folded my arms in front of me as he walked right over to Sky and asked, "What are you doing?"

"I'm trying to enjoy my date. What does it look like?"

"Date?" He looked over at me as I frowned. "With him? He looks old enough to be your dad. You tripping Sky."

He looked familiar to me. I'd seen this dude before. "Weslan, the last time I checked, I was a grown ass woman. Who I date is none of your business."

He looked over at me and shook his head. If I wasn't mistaken, I could see in his eyes that he recognized me, too. I couldn't figure out where I'd seen him, but I was willing to bet that he'd copped from me back in the day. That was why he wasn't really pressing the issue. "Whatever. Call me later. For real."

She rolled her eyes and turned back to me. "I'm sorry."

"It's cool. How old is your brother? He looks familiar."

"He's almost forty. That's why he thinks he's my dad."

"Hmm. Okay, so umm... can I spend more time with you?" I asked as I pulled her closer to me by her hips.

"Hell yeah," she said softly against my lips. "Follow me."

I kissed her lips, then walked to my car. Her brother was still chilling in the cut, though. He was crazy if he thought I didn't see him. From my days on the street, I was always aware of my surroundings. When I got in my ride, I followed Sky as he watched and fell in line behind me.

$$\maltese \quad 8 \quad \maltese$$

S ky

"MAKE YOURSELF COMFORTABLE. I'M GONNA GO CHANGE."

"A'ight."

I walked to my bedroom as Colson sat on the couch. Damn he turned me on. The way he stood there in that protective stance when my brother ran up on us was sexy as hell. Although Weslan didn't say so, it looked like he recognized Colson from somewhere, too. As I took off my jewelry, I couldn't help but wonder about Colson's past. He said that particular day I'd asked wasn't the day, so it had to be something bad.

Shaking my head of my thoughts of the possibilities, I concentrated on who he was now. He was a boss, handling his businesses with ease. His shit had to be intact for him to take as much time away as he did. He was the type of stability I needed in my life. It helped that he was fine as hell. I was tired of the men my age, not having the total package. They had the physical, but their lives would be in chaos. Either that or they just didn't have their shit together. At almost thirty years old, that was unacceptable.

After putting on some tights and a long t-shirt, I joined Colson on the couch. He immediately grabbed my legs and pulled them in his lap. When he started massaging them, my head dropped back, and my eyes closed as a moan left my lips. He kneaded them to perfection, and then he went to my feet. I swear he had to have missed his calling to be a masseuse. After massaging my feet for a moment, he made his way back up my legs. Once he got to my mid-thigh, he stopped. My eyes opened slowly to see him staring at me.

Just as I was about to swing my feet to the floor, he held my legs still. "You don't have to move them, unless you just want to."

"Well, I thought you might want a drink or something."

"What's or something?"

"I don't know... whatever else there is that you want," I said slowly.

Colson released my legs, and then scooted closer to me. "Does the 'or something' include these lips?" he asked, then leaned in and kissed me softly.

"Possibly," I whispered.

He leaned in and kissed me again, this time a little stronger, sliding his tongue inside slowly. My hands slid up his face as I pulled him in deeper. The moan that left my lips resonated inside of him as I leaned back, pulling him with me. His hands explored my body, memorizing its contours. When they reached my breasts, my nipples rose to greet him through the t-shirt. Separating his mouth from mine, Colson opened his eyes to stare at me. He played with the hem of my garment, as if I held the power to make him whole, then he slid his hand beneath it.

I didn't put on a bra. I never wore one at home. Colson's hand caressed my stomach, and when he grabbed the extra flesh that was there, that shit did something to me. My eyes were still on his as my lips parted. He eased his body over mine as his hands eased up my body to toy with my nipple. That was all it took for me to lift my legs and wrap them around his waist, giving him the green light to do with me as he pleased. I'd never been so desperate to feel anybody within my walls as I was feeling for Colson.

He didn't make a sound as he moved to my neck, kissing it tenderly, as I grabbed at his shirt. Slowly, he sank his teeth into my flesh, and I moaned loudly. Stopping momentarily to free himself of his shirt, he pulled me up to a sitting position and pulled my shirt over my head. "Damn, you're beautiful," he said, then brought his mouth to my nipple.

As he feasted, his other hand eased between my legs, grabbing me by the pussy, almost making me cum on myself. "Colson... God!"

"I've been called that before, but I promise you, I ain't Him."

Oh, this cocky muthafucka. Just his words heated me up immensely, and I believed that he felt that shit. Bringing his other hand to my breasts, he pushed them together and began sucking my nipples simultaneously. My body jerked in response, and I couldn't stop the sweetness that oozed between my legs. "Fuuuck!"

Feeling my legs trembling, he brought his lips to my earlobe and bit it gently. "Did you cum for me, baby?"

"Yeeeessss!"

Colson pulled my tights down, lifting my hips on his own. He kissed his way up my birthmark, and then slid his fingers inside of me, stroking my G-spot for a moment, then pulled them out and brought them to his lips. The way he slurped my juices from his fingers had me on the verge of cumming again. As if reading my thoughts, he said, "Let me make that pussy scream my name again. Can I do that?"

"Fuck, yes!"

"Ms. Jones, to say you a teacher, you shol' have a dirty mouth."

"Mmm. Are you the principal? You gon' write me up?"

"Since you're my subordinate, I think I need to enforce corporal punishment."

Colson turned me over to my side and smacked my ass, causing me to hiss in excitement. Lifting my leg straight up in the air, he brought his lips to my lower lips and wrapped them around my clit. "I love this big, juicy-ass clit," he said right against it.

The goosebumps filled every inch of my flesh, sensitizing my entire body to his presence as he licked me from here to kingdom come. And it felt like I'd died and gone to heaven when he began sucking my clit. Sliding his fingers inside of me again, he stroked my spot, making me squirm in anticipation. "Colson... shit! I'm about to cum again!"

Suddenly, he stopped. I felt like crying. "Do you have a condom, baby?"

"Noooooo! Colson! I can't go to bed like this. Shiiiit!"

"Do you trust me?"

"I can't think about the consequences right now of what could happen... just give it to me. Pleeeeaaasse!"

The more I screamed, the more he seemed to get turned on. He stood from the sofa and his eyes seemed to go dark like a damn shark as he took off his pants. His shit was hanging between his legs, begging to get wet. He stroked it a few times as he stared at me, lying on my side, legs wide open for him. I wanted to whine like a toddler and have a fucking tantrum. I needed to be put out of my misery. By the look on his face, I knew he was finna slay my shit, though. I laid there breathing heavily, my eyes travelling the length of his dick, trying my best to summon him to me. I could feel the juices leaking out of me, so I put my hand down there and began stroking myself.

Colson licked his lips as he watched me. But when I brought my fingers to my mouth, that did it. He came to me hastily and shoved his dick inside of me like there was a fire to put out. Shit... there was, and by the feel of it, his hose was the one for the fucking job. Pushing my leg to the side, Colson dug up in my shit like there was no tomorrow. "Fuuuck!! Yes, Colson! Fuck me!"

He slapped my ass while digging me out. That muthafucka was

so damned deep, he was probably gonna put my cervix in my hand when he finished. As he went deeper, I put my hand on his abs, trying to keep him from destroying my shit. "Nah. You was begging for this shit. Calling on the Lord. Now, He done answered your prayer and you wanna run the other way. You better thank Him for his fast response, Sky."

No this muthafucka didn't. I couldn't even respond, though. He was fucking the wind out of me, while he was all nonchalant sounding. I looked back at him and saw the deep frown on his face. "Colson... tell me how my pussy feels, baby."

"Shit. It feels like payday, baby. Good as fuck."

He leaned over my body and went even deeper as he kissed the back of my shoulder. *God! How much dick he had?* "Sky... fuuuck..."

His grunts and deep groans made my orgasm greet him without warning, and I screamed out my pleasure as he fucked me harder, grabbing ahold of my breast for leverage. "Sky, tell me you mine."

"Oooh Colson, this pussy is all yours."

"Naw. I want more than the pussy. I want all of you. So tell me."

"You can claim ownership of all of me, Colson. Shit!"

He again lifted my leg, forcing me to turn over to my back and draped it over his shoulder. While he wore me out a few minutes ago, he was the total opposite now. It felt like he was making love to my spirit. His mouth found mine as he gently rubbed my nipples. Wrapping my other leg around his waist, he wound that dick into me expertly, showing me his experience on the pipeline. He was laying that pipe perfectly. Colson stared into my eyes as he allowed his chest to rub against my nipples, while his dick grazed my clit with every stroke. I was on the verge of cumming again. "Sky... you about to drain me, baby."

"Good. You doing... that shit to me, tooooo!" I screamed as I came again.

Colson frowned and bit his bottom lip. When my tremors

eased a little, he pulled out and came on my stomach. He came a damn river, which either meant that he did that all the time or he hadn't had sex in a while. Either way, this was the best sex I'd ever had on a fucking sofa. "You got some good pussy... fuuuck!"

Now my conscience wanted to kick in. Not only did I barely know this man, but I'd let him fuck me raw and told him that I was his. At this point, there was nothing I could do about fucking him raw but pray he was clean. He stood and smiled at me. "Where is your bathroom so I can get a towel to clean you up?"

"Down the hall to the left," I said while still panting.

My pussy was throbbing after the shit he put on me, and I could already see myself making weekend trips to Houston to get it. When he came back, he licked his lips as he stared at me for a moment, then wiped the cum from my stomach. Grabbing my hand after he did, he lifted me to my wobbly legs. Chuckling softly, he lifted me in his arms like a baby. Another turn on. I was a big girl and I needed a man that could handle all of me, and he did that shit with ease. "Point me in the direction of your bedroom, baby."

After directing him down the hall, I laid my head on his chest. A soft moan left me as I thought about how mind-blowing the sex was, and I knew I had only scratched the surface of how he could make me feel. I'd lost all my fucking inhibitions and I hoped I didn't have to pay for that shit later. When he placed me in the bed, I instantly opened my legs, wanting him to fill me once again. He chuckled and rubbed his hand down his beard. "Sky, just tell me what you want. I'm here to oblige, baby."

"Everything?"

"Yeah..." he said hesitantly.

"After you come over here and make love to me again, I wanna know everything I should about you since I'm yours now."

He glanced at the floor for a moment, then lifted his eyes to mine. His under eye gaze was dark again, and I didn't know what to make of it, other than it was turning me on even more so. When I first met him, he looked so professional and all about his business, but right now, he looked like one of those dangerous thugs I'd only seen on TV. "A'ight. I got'chu. And that goes both ways."

Although he said that, I believed he already knew everything he needed to know about me, because there wasn't much to tell. We'd had in depth conversation about ourselves. What I didn't tell him about me, I was sure he'd already figured it out. When he made his way to me, my body was trembling in anticipation. Just as I thought, he pleased me orally, making me cum twice. The hurting he put on my body with that anaconda, though, took me out the game... like literally. I was screaming so much, I lost my damn voice. He was so rough, and I liked that shit. When he straddled my legs from the back and leaned over to my ear, he'd said, *"Fuck all that screaming and cum for daddy."*

My body did as he commanded on the fucking spot. And that was the last damn thing I remembered, because I passed smooth the fuck out.

# ❧ 9 ❧

C olson

I LAID IN THE BED AND LISTENED TO SKY LIGHTLY SNORE AS I chuckled. She had me fucked up if she thought she'd be able to hold a full conversation when I finished with her. I'd had her every way imaginable, and I still wanted more. After that last orgasm, she passed smooth out. Her head had barely hit the pillow. That was hilarious to me. It wasn't the first time I'd seen a woman do that, but this was my first time being with a woman as young as her, so I assumed she'd hang with me. As I watched her sleep, I could only think about how fulfilling my life would be with her in it.

I was willing to tell her everything, but I hoped she was willing to accept that part of me. She'd gotten a glimpse of him during sex. I became this animalistic, dark person during sex, because I looked at the woman as my prey. But something came over me during our session, and I became gentler, wanting to make love to her. Something told me she was feeling the thug inside of me, though. Glancing at the time, I saw it was almost one in the morning. I didn't plan to spend the night, but it looked like that was exactly what was gonna happen, because I wouldn't dare leave while she was sleeping, and I didn't wanna wake her up, either.

As I continued to admire everything about Sky, my phone started ringing. I rolled my eyes as I jumped up from the bed, trying to silence it before it woke her up. It was an unknown number, and I wasn't for the shit tonight, not after the amazing time I'd had with Sky. After I sat it down on her nightstand, I turned to look at Sky to find her looking at me. "I'm sorry. I was trying to silence it before it woke you up."

"It's okay. When did I fall asleep?"

"After you had that last mind-blowing orgasm. That shit took you right on out, baby."

She giggled, then held her arms out for me to join her. I slid in next to her as I bit my bottom lip. Slowly sliding my finger down the side of her face, I said, "It feels good to call you mine, Sky. So damn good."

I pulled her on top of me and stared in her eyes. "It does feel amazing, Colson."

I wrapped my arms around her as she laid her head on my chest. "Colson?"

"Yeah baby?"

"You used to sell drugs, huh?"

I swallowed hard. I didn't know how she came to that conclusion, but I had to answer her. "Yeah. I did."

"For how long? And when did you stop?"

"I started when I was fourteen years old. I stopped when I got busted."

"Busted? You went to prison?" she asked as she lifted her head to look in my eyes.

"Yeah, for three years. Does that make you look at me any differently?"

"No. The only way it would was if you still did that shit."

"Once I got out of prison, I knew I had to do better. Next time, I wouldn't be so lucky and just get jail time. Every time I graced those streets, I was putting my life in danger."

"That's very true. So, you were on the streets for twenty years?"

"Yeah, almost... like eighteen or nineteen. Honestly, I think that's how I know your brother. I didn't just push the hard shit. I sold kush, too."

"Aww shit. I could see that he recognized you. My mama caught him smoking that when he was in high school. She beat his ass."

I chuckled. "Well, that didn't stop it, because I don't think it was that long before I got locked up."

"No, he hasn't stopped. He still smokes that shit. That's why his ass couldn't finish school. He was always high. Seeing how it affected him, I opted to stay away from it."

"Good for you. It affects people differently. Some people can smoke it recreationally and it doesn't bother them, while other people get hooked and crave more... searching for their next high. I don't smoke it often, because I got used to not sampling my own product."

Before she could ask anything else, my phone started vibrating on her nightstand again. I exhaled loudly and rolled my eyes. Grabbing it, I noticed it was from the same number as before. I decided to answer it this time, because I didn't want Sky to think I was avoiding some woman. "Hello?"

"Cole... I need you. I think I fucked up."

Rolling my eyes again, I said, "What else is new? What did you do this time, Val?"

"I smoked all Jeremy shit. He gon' kill my ass."

"Well, in case he does, I love you, big sis. I wish you would have left that shit alone while you had time. Mama loves you, too, and she would do anything for you, but you ruined your life, sis."

"You a cold muthafucka, Cole! I hate yo' ass!"

"That ain't nothing new, either. Get yo' shit together, Val. I tried to help you, but you gotta want to help yo'self."

I ended the call and sat my phone on the nightstand as Sky watched me. She didn't say anything for a while until I looked at her. "You okay, Colson?"

"Yeah. Ain't shit finna ruin my time with you. I have a meeting Monday and rounds to make Tuesday, so I won't be able to come see you until Wednesday. And that's if you don't have anything to do."

"We have staff meetings on Wednesdays."

"See? So, why would I let that kill the little time we have left?"

"I know. How are we gonna maintain our relationship if we can only see one another on the weekends?"

"I don't always have meetings. So, I'll come see you as often as I can. I promise. We still have a lot to get to know about each other. Like where you're ticklish at," I said as I began to tickle her.

She screamed with laughter as she tried to fight me off her. Baby girl was strong as hell, too. Of course, the tickling led to other things. Before I knew it, I was on top of her, drilling that good pussy of hers. I couldn't get enough. It was like she had been waiting for me to find her and God placed us at the right place at the right time to find one another. My heart felt open when it concerned her, and I hadn't felt that way in a long time. There was this chick before I went to jail that was supposed to be my rider, but as soon as a nigga got locked up, she skipped town.

Then there was one not long after I got out, and another when I was forty-five. None of them gave me the feeling Sky did. Although she was young, I felt like she was just who I needed. I wanted a kid or two. A woman my age most likely couldn't or wouldn't give me that. So, Sky Sade Agnes Jones was just the woman for me, and I didn't care who had a problem with it. After we'd finished our countless rounds of sex and had caught our breath, Sky called out, "Colson?"

"Yeah?"

"I could see your dark side in your eyes. I was just waiting on you to tell me. I don't care what you used to do. I only care about the present. That's it."

"What about the future?"

"I care about that, too, but it's not at the forefront of my mind right now."

I couldn't wait to make her start thinking about the future. It was already on my mind and we hadn't known one another for a week yet.

◈

"What do the numbers say?"

"The numbers say the store is doing well, but we have so many complaints."

"I'm not shutting the store down, Andrew. We can go in and weed some of the employees out that are providing horrible customer service, but as long as the numbers are good, I'm not shutting it down. They barely build anything of substance in the hood already. Greenspoint Mall area needs that Smoothie King. So, put together a plan for customer service training and make sure the cameras are working so I can see exactly what's going on."

"Yes, sir."

"What else y'all got for me? I know I have a conference at the end of next month, but that's it."

"I wouldn't mind if you would join me for a staff meeting at my store."

I looked around to see a raised hand in the back of the crowd. It was one of my more timid managers. The employees somewhat ran over him. "When is it, Greg?"

"It's Wednesday at five."

"Okay. I'll be there. Don't tell your employees that I'm coming."

As the managers moved on to the next topic of discussion, my phone vibrated. When I saw the text message was from Sky, I opened it to see, *I miss you.*

That made me smile. Knowing that she accepted me, flaws and all, was a turn on like no other. She just seemed so perfect. She was raised right, didn't get into trouble, was a straight A student in school and was now a teacher, trying to make a difference in the lives of these hoodlums called children. On top of all that, she was a freak. Although she was trying to keep that side of her on lock, I brought all that shit out the other night. She was so damn fine. I responded, *I miss you, too, baby.*

Someone cleared their throat, and when I looked up, they were all trying to hide their grins. "No offense Mr. Crook, but only a woman can put that kind of smile on a man's face."

One of the female managers turned red, and my only black female manager rolled her eyes and crossed her legs. She always said the rest of them were a bunch of ass kissers, and I'd just laugh at her. She and I always had an open line of communication. I wanted her to succeed against the odds, so I helped her more in the beginning. She wasn't really qualified for the job, so rumors were flying, and her husband had even questioned me respectfully.

She was the only black woman that had applied for a management position, and out of all my stores, I didn't have one. So, for diversity purposes, I hired her, making sure she understood that she wasn't qualified. I'd told her if she worked her ass off, she could be extremely successful. That was five years ago, and she had one of the most successful and well-ran stores in Houston. After I didn't verbally respond to his statement, he cleared his throat again and reiterated, "We were wondering if we would be getting incentives again this year."

"You are, but the criteria is changing. I'm glad you brought that up. One of the criteria will be that health inspections have to be at least a ninety-five. It's no excuse to justify a filthy store. If inspections of equipment are made daily, then repairs or maintenance can be scheduled in a timely manner. Also, encourage customers to leave reviews. I'll be looking over those as well. Anything under a four-star average for the year will be further reviewed. If the rating can't be explained, then that store won't receive the incentive. You can also offer coupons for customers that review. I'll get with the marketing team to generate the coupon when a review is left on the website."

There were a couple of frowns, but of course they were from the ones that weren't far from the chopping block anyway. Most of them were taking notes, though. I continued. "I will also be implementing mystery shoppers. And you'll never know when I may decide to pop in. I think that's it regarding the incentives. The other aspects of it will remain. Any questions?"

No one said a word as my phone vibrated again. "Okay, if there's nothing else, you're dismissed."

We all gathered our things to get ready to leave. I looked at my phone to see I'd gotten a picture message. When I opened it, I chuckled. It was a picture of Sky with her lips poked out. She was seated at her desk. It was so hard leaving her yesterday. I'd hugged and kissed her multiple times before I actually left. I wished she was in Houston. I had another meeting with the marketing team, and I'd be done for the day. After seriously contemplating going to Beaumont, I walked out of the conference room with a smile on my face.

When I got to the foyer of the hotel, I sent Sky another message. *Do you have a busy evening?* Then, I got on Proflowers to have a bouquet delivered to her at school later this week. "She must be really special to have you zoning out in meetings. That never happens."

I looked up from my phone to see Cynthia, my only black female manager, talking to me with a grin on her face. "She is. It hasn't been long, but I can feel that she's it. I'm gonna take it slow, though."

"Sounds like me and Mel. We met and within a week, we were a couple damn near in love."

"Shit. I know the feeling. I'm feeling the fuck out of her. It's barely been a week since we met, and I can't stop thinking about her."

"Well, I wish you the best of luck then. Hopefully, we'll get to meet her soon."

"Hopefully."

She walked away to her car as I got in my Escalade. My phone vibrated, letting me know that I'd received a text. Sky's name was on the screen, and her message read, *No. I wish I did... a busy evening with you. Why? You coming to see me?*

Not long after I finished reading, she called. I frowned slightly and looked to see it was almost noon. She was probably on her lunch. "Hey, beautiful."

"Hey, handsome. You coming to Beaumont?"

"I don't know for sure yet, but I want to."

"Don't push it. I know you have a full day. I just miss you."

"I miss you, too, baby. If I can make it, I'm gonna come down and leave in the morning. Go eat your lunch and call me when you get off."

"Okay. Talk to you soon."

"A'ight, baby."

I ended the call, wishing I could just hop in my vehicle and go to her. Damn. Unfortunately, we were both grown, handling grownup responsibilities. But I could see how people could forget about the things that were necessary when they were excited about someone they'd met.

Once I'd gotten lunch, ran a few errands, personal and business, I headed home. Looking at the time to see it was only five, I decided I would take a shower and head to Sky. I should be able to make it to Beaumont by seven. *Who was this nigga I'd become?* She literally made me chase her and want to see her every waking moment. When she'd called earlier and she talked about how tired she was, I wanted to be able to give her a massage and let her fall asleep on my chest. Just to be able to provide her some comfort was the first thing that came to mind. While I loved sex with her, it wasn't my first thought whenever I thought about her.

That was beyond unusual, because it seemed we hadn't known one another long enough to really know one another at all. I already cared for her, hence the reason I was so quick to wanna make her mine. With my history, even caring for a woman was a big deal. Her confidence and beauty was so damn attractive it grabbed ahold of me and refused to let go. But that was a good thing, because I had no plans of letting go, either.

## 🌿 10 🌿

S<sup>ky</sup>

"WHY DON'T YOU DO ME A FAVOR AND GO ON TO THE OFFICE? I don't have the time nor the energy to deal with your attitude and disrespect today."

"I ain't the one with an attitude. You need to get that shit in check."

"Mya, please leave, now. I don't want to have to call the officer in here. You're being disruptive and I needed you to leave ten minutes ago."

She smacked her lips and flipped the desk over as she stood and walked out the class. Closing my eyes for a moment, I tried to figure out how this day had gotten away from me. I was in an exceptional mood after lunch, but it seemed to go downhill from there. As I got the class to settle down, I tried to continue with the day's lesson, but I just didn't have it in me after that. Mya had been disruptive since she'd first walked through the door. These kids were getting out of hand, and it was making being a teacher a daily struggle.

I'd made calls to parents, talked to the kids one on one, and written referrals, but it was like nothing was helping. I was tired. How could I effectively make a difference with kids that didn't even respect me enough to sit there and learn something? It wasn't all of them, but dear God, it was most of them. I didn't know how the kids that wanted to learn something could retain anything with the chaos that ensued sometimes. Every day wasn't like this, but the ones that were made me rethink my whole career choice. There were rarely any exceptional days, which made it hard to level things out.

It was like we had to be more concerned with behavior instead of teaching, and at this point, it was almost a lost cause. I taught mostly eleventh graders and seniors. If their behavior was still a constant problem at that age, most likely, there was nothing we as teachers could do about it. What made things even harder was that some of the parents were just as hard to deal with as the kids. I was gonna be thirty in a couple of weeks. I never expected to feel exhausted with my job this soon. As I stood at the board, I sat the dry erase marker down and sat at my desk while the kids started talking again.

Trying to remain positive in situations like this was so fucking hard. It was the second day after spring break. I should have known that things would be rough this week. Their minds were still on break. I was just glad this was my last class of the day. We only had fifteen minutes left, and at least twenty minutes of the class was me going back and forth with students. I'd kicked three of them out. That was unacceptable. Dropping my head to my hands, I sat that way for a moment, then ran my hands down my face. I rushed today to come to this shit.

I'd woken up late, forgoing putting on makeup, just to get here on time. And for what? To be frustrated to the point of throwing in the towel. One of the students approached my desk. She was one of the 'good' kids in my last class. "Ms. Jones, you okay?"

"Yeah. Just frustrated. Thanks."

She nodded and went back to her desk, not so secretly watching me for the remaining of the class period. When that bell rang, I never felt as happy as I did at that moment. Grabbing my things, I silently prayed for a better day tomorrow. I hightailed my ass out of there before anyone could stop me to talk. I couldn't deal with nothing more from West Brook High School today.

Once I got in my car, I called Colson to let him know I was on my way home. We weren't on the phone long since he was at the bank. Today was a day I could use one of his massages. When I got to my house, I sat in the driveway for a moment, thinking about today and rolling my eyes. I needed a damn drink. I got out of my car and made my way inside as my brother drove in the driveway. I rolled my eyes. It had already been a day. I didn't need his bullshit, too. "Hey, Sky. How was your day?"

"Hey, Wes. It was a little stressful. How was your day?"

"It was good. You got time to talk to me?"

"Yeah. Come in."

I opened the door and he followed me inside as I sat my things down and turned on a couple of lights. Bracing myself for the bullshit, I immediately went to my liquor cabinet and pulled out a bottle of Paul Masson. "So, instead of immediately trying to discipline you like a kid, I should have asked how you and 'Cole as shit' met."

I frowned, and then my eyebrows lifted. "How do you know him?"

"He used to sell me dime bags 'til he got busted."

I turned away from him and took a swig of my drink from the bottle. "Has he changed? Or is he still on the streets?"

"He owns quite a few Smoothie Kings. I'm so glad that he told me about his past already or I would have been hot as shit right now."

"When did y'all meet?"

"In Galveston a week ago."

"And he's already told you about that shit?"

"Yes. That's not a good thing?"

"Yeah. It is. I'm just surprised. He's definitely not who he used to be. I still don't totally trust it, though, sis."

"Well, it's a good thing our relationship isn't built on your trust issues."

"You feeling him like that?"

"Yes. And I need you to respect that. I'm almost thirty years old. If I need you in that capacity, I'll holler. But I think I can handle that."

"Sis, you don't know that nigga like you think you do. I done seen him body niggas over five dollars. He's ruthless."

"Good. Then I should feel safe and protected whenever I'm with him, since I'm definitely worth more than five dollars. Are you done?"

He looked pissed, but he'd get over it. I knew he wouldn't dare say all this shit to Colson's face or Cole as shit's face, as he called him. He snatched his keys from the countertop as I took another swig of my Paul Masson straight from the bottle. "Don't call me when he hurts you, because I've warned you. I've seen this nigga straight up use women. But that's who you want, go for it."

"Weslan, that shit was fucking twenty years ago!"

"Yeah, it was, and yo' ass was nine! Let that sink in."

He walked out the door, and I slammed it behind him. I just wanted to say fuck it all and become a damn hermit. Grabbing my bottle, I went to the bathroom and ran some bath water. It was only four o'clock, and I was ready to get fucked up and go to sleep. Going to my room, I stripped out of my clothes and went back to the bathroom. After taking another swig, I sat on side of the tub. *Was Colson abusive like Wes was trying to insinuate?* That shit didn't matter. Everything he was saying about him was in the past. I wasn't about to fall into the accusatory trap. Whatever I wanted to know, I would ask him.

After turning the water off, I sank into the tub. I'd practically killed half the bottle of Paul Masson and I was feeling that shit. Taking a deep breath, I laid back and thought about all the things I wanted to ask Colson. Then I thought about how my day had gone and I started crying. As much as I loved being a teacher, I was starting to hate my job. All the bullshit I believed when I was brand new was going out the window. I was starting to lose hope in these kids I was teaching and that wasn't a good feeling.

Once I drunkenly washed myself, I let the water out, then rinsed off. I had to have been in the tub for at least an hour. I was drunk as hell. Thankfully, it was still early where I could sleep it off. Noticing it was damn near seven o'clock, I had to rethink that. Maybe I should call-in sick tomorrow or just take a personal day. No. *I'm gonna take a mental health day.* We had those now. That wasn't a lie. I needed to renew my shit, 'cause I was ready to quit my job like I didn't have all these damn bills.

After drying off, I stumbled all the way to my bed and fell right in it, belching and laughing. This shit was ridiculous. As I tried to get better situated, my damned doorbell rang. I was sure Weslan had brought his ass back to apologize. He usually did. Snatching my robe from the hook on the door, I almost bust my ass. I laughed my way all the way to the door. When I got to it, I hushed myself by putting my finger over my lips. "Who is it?" I asked, and then hiccupped.

I slapped my hand over my mouth as the bass voice said, "Colson."

*Oh shit!* I stood up straight and tried to overcome my drunken state through a pep talk, then opened the door. He was smiling, but it faded a bit as he looked at me. "Hey!" I said and grabbed his hand, pulling him inside.

"Hey," he said kind of dryly. "What's up with you?"

"I had a horrible day. My last class had me wanting to change careers, and then Wes came here talking shit about you. I just needed to have something to drink to forget about all that shit for tonight."

He pulled me in his arms. "Listen. If you need to just get away, you can always call me. I'll stop whatever I'm doing to come to you. If you wanna drive out to me sometimes, just let me know. But don't do this shit no more while you're alone. What if you fell and really hurt yourself? This shit is dangerous."

He grabbed my chin and forced me to stare in his eyes. "I'm sorry," I said softly. "I was in bed. I had no plans of getting back up. You didn't call, so I didn't think you were coming."

"Don't worry, baby. I got'chu."

He led me back to my bedroom after locking the door, then asked, "What kind of shit yo' brother had to say about me?"

"That you were a womanizer."

"I was back then. Why he bringing up shit from twenty years ago?"

"Same thing I asked as I let my robe slip from my shoulders." Colson stared at my body unashamedly. "He also said that you had killed a nigga for owing you five dollars."

He dropped his head, looking at the floor, then gave me that sexy-ass under eyed stare. "That scare you, baby?"

"If five dollars meant that much to you, what would you do to protect me?"

I laid on the bed on my back and opened my legs for him as he dropped his duffle bag. "It wasn't about the amount of money. It was about him disrespecting me. He owed a debt, and to assume I didn't need or want my money was the wrong assumption. Now, for you? If I had to, I'd burn all of Beaumont down to protect you. Rub that pussy for me, baby. Make it juicy for me," he said as he took his shirt off.

His words had me wet already. I'd heard drunken sex was the best sex, and now I was about to find out. "Colson?" I called out as I finger fucked myself, watching him take his pants off.

"Yeah?"

"You say what'chu mean and mean what'chu say, right? You wouldn't fuck over me, huh? You wouldn't hurt me in no way, would you?"

He didn't answer me right away. He slid in bed, hovering over me. "Look at me, so we can dead this." When I looked at him through the slits of my low eyes, he continued as I continued pleasuring myself. "You the woman I want. I'm too old for bullshit ass games. If I'm wit'chu, I ain't with nobody else. I hope you feeling me, so I don't have to repeat that shit. I ain't ever been one to lie. I never had a reason to. I left all that stupid shit in my thirties. Everything I do to you, physically, mentally and emotionally will feel like a fucking orgasm. I wanna give you spiritual orgasms and have you craving a nigga like these lying ass fiends out her. You got me?"

I moaned softly as my eyes closed. Colson slid his hand to my neck, gripping it gently but firmly and asked again, "I asked if you got me?"

"I got'chu, Cole."

"You can call me whatever you want, but don't call me Cole. That's reserved for fuck niggas and backstabbing family."

"Can I call you by your middle name? Jermaine?"

"Whatever else you want."

With that, he moved my hand to the side and pushed inside of me as he sucked my damn fingers dry. Every nerve in my shit felt like it was turned inside out as he fed me the dick. I was softly screaming his name, arching my back and scratching his. Grabbing his bald head, I ran my nails over it and saw the goosebumps appear on his flesh. Colson wanted only me, and Wes could kiss my ass. *Wait... did he call Wes a fiend?*

## ❧ 11 ❧

C olson

IF SKY'S PUSSY WAS A HOUSE, THIS SHIT WOULD BE A MANSION in Dubai.

If it was food, it would be the most expensive caviar.

If it was clothes, it would be hand-woven silk.

If it was jewels, it would be a flawless ruby.

Her pussy had me by the nuts, and no matter how rough I wanted to be, her shit humbled me every time. After she pulled that first nut from me, I slid right back in her shit. I stroked her slow and deep, feeling the wetness coat my dick and hearing her shit talk to me. Everything about it had me captivated, wowed by its excellence, and frozen in time to feel its essence. My manhood craved her femininity... her softness that was the exact opposite of me. I'd been hard all my life, but Sky made me feel. My walls could come down and I could be me when I was with her. Seeing her drunk and alone scared the fuck out of me. Losing her would kill me inside, because she might as well had been the last woman on earth.

As I fulfilled both our desires, taking our bodies to places neither had ever seen, her doorbell rang. I frowned and her eyes popped open. "You expecting somebody?" I asked as I continued to stroke her.

Dipping my head to her neck, I kissed her softly as she whispered, "No. Please, don't stop."

Her words caused me to dive deeper into her, soothing her spirit and all her worries. I could feel her releasing all that shit, but some dumbass was at the door threatening all that. As she arched her back, I pulled her nipple in my mouth. Her cries and moans as she came took me there with her, and I released inside of her as I heard the door open. "What the fuck?"

I hopped off her and pulled my gun from my duffle bag and slid my drawers on as she tried to sit up in the bed. I opened her bedroom door and the barrel of my gun was face to face with her brother. "Shit!" he said raising his hands.

I refused to lower my gun until he said, "My bad. I was coming to check on Sky because she was drinking when I left."

"Yeah, you was busy running down my resume, right?"

"I was tryna protect my little sister."

"Protect her by tearing me down? I'm gon' tell you this. Don't speak on shit you don't have a clue about. Keep your opinions to your damn self."

When I turned to glance at Sky, I noticed she'd gone to sleep. "She needed to know who she was dealing with."

"That's cool and all, but respect what we have and quit being a fuck nigga. I got her, and I ain't going nowhere if she don't want me to. I started remembering exactly who you was, and I don't want to have to let her know who she's dealing with, either. Feel me?"

He didn't answer, so I lifted my gun again, and his hands flew in the air. "I got'chu."

"Good. Now leave so we can sleep in peace."

I followed his punk ass to the door and locked it. He had better been glad that he was her brother. He would have gotten fucked up just now. After seeing him drive away from the window, I made my way back to the bedroom with Sky. Her ass was knocked the fuck out. That was good, though, because she needed to sleep that shit off if she was going to make it to work tomorrow. It was only nine-thirty. I knew she had to be leaving early. If she didn't have to work, I'd stay until eight-thirty. I didn't plan on popping in on any of the stores until ten or later. When I got back to the room, I put my gun back in my bag and slid in the bed with Sky.

I lifted her to where I could hold her in my arms. Baby girl was damn near dead. She never even flinched when I moved her. That Paul Masson had fucked her ass all the way up without lube. That shit snuck up on her ass, I bet. For some people, it did that shit. She was obviously one of them. Looking at how much of that shit she drank, if that bottle was full, she'd killed more than half of it. Slowly shaking my head, I kissed her forehead, then rolled to my back. When she started sweating, her ass was gon' have to get off my arm.

Thinking about all the shit her brother probably told her had infuriated me. Some people couldn't accept the change in others. They always used their past against them or to define them. That was my life in a fucking nutshell. People like him were the reason I left this area. I couldn't get a fresh start with people. Turning to my side to look at Sky again, she was breathing heavily as I pushed her hair from her face. She was so beautiful, and I couldn't wait to fall for her. That was one thing about being older. I knew exactly what I wanted and how it should feel. Sky Sade Agnes Jones was what and who I wanted, and I felt her in my soul.

As I stared at her, gently rubbing her face, her eyes fluttered open. She smiled softly at me, and then went to her knees in the bed. She looked like she could barely hold herself up, so I wasn't sure where she was trying to go or what she was trying to do until her leg swung across my body. My dick automatically stiffened for her. As I got ready to feel her warmness coat me, she changed the game up and slid down my body, her nipples rubbing me down until she was face to face with the one-eyed monster. She didn't waste any time. When her mouth covered it, she instantly deep-throated it, causing me to sit the fuck up and watch her technique.

As I propped myself on my elbows, watching the natural lubricant leave her mouth, I wanted to bust already. Feeling her mouth make love to my dick was everything, and she knew what the hell she was doing, too. Leaning forward, I grabbed a handful of her hair. I swear that professional nigga she met in Galveston was long gone. Thanks to her brother, the old me was surfacing, and I was ready to fuck some shit up, starting with the back of her throat.

I slowly began thrusting in her mouth, just to see how far I could go. Nothing about me was small... shoe size fourteen, six-feet-five-inches tall, and a ten-inch monster between my legs. My hands could practically palm her entire face. When I found my limits, I teased that shit, causing her to gag a bit. I knew I'd better be careful since she was drunk. I couldn't have her throwing up on me. When she suctioned on my shit, I lost my focus. All thrusting ceased as my grip on her hair tightened. *Fuck!* I bit my bottom lip and frowned as I drowned in pleasure. "Fuck, Sky!"

My nut shot out me, in search of the back of her throat. It didn't make it right away. She lifted her head, allowing it to run down her chin. I think I liked the drunk Sky. Damn. Swallowing what was in her mouth, she mounted me and rode the fuck outta my dick. Naw... her ass wasn't going nowhere. She was mine forever. I wrapped my arms around her waist and began giving it to her drunk ass. "Colson!! Shiiiit!"

She was screaming like I was killing her. I guess I was... killing that pussy only to revive it later. Feeling her juices leak to my balls only propelled me forward. I growled and grunted as my nut rose to the surface, giving me that high that I wanted to get used to feeling with her. She began trembling and cursing, letting me know that her orgasm had arrived, and I couldn't help but join her with the choke hold her pussy had on me.

We laid there, panting like crazy. I kissed her forehead, then she rolled over and went back to sleep. This time, I joined her... sticky and all.

⚜

"SKY, YOU GON' BE LATE TO WORK, BABY. IT'S SIX-THIRTY."

I'd just woken up and Sky was still knocked the hell out. She lifted her head slowly and moaned. "I took a mental health day today."

Wiping her eyes, she picked at the dry cum on her chin with a frown on her face. I chuckled while she tried to figure out what it was. "What's so funny?"

"Watching you scratch my kids off your chin."

Her eyes widened and she hopped up from the bed and almost fell. I got up with her as I continued to laugh. When I got to the bathroom, she was washing her face. It was red as hell, too. I didn't know what she was embarrassed for. She glanced over at me, then lowered her face to the towel. Grabbing her by the wrist, I pulled her to me. "What'chu embarrassed for? That shit nearly turned my ass out last night."

She lifted her eyes to mine. Sky couldn't have been more than five-foot-seven or eight, so she really had to look up at me. I picked her up and sat her on the countertop as my dick hardened just thinking about the nasty shit she did to me. "I don't want you to think I'ma hoe. I've been doing shit lately with you that takes me months to do with anyone else."

"But I ain't anyone else. Just go with the flow. You think I eat pussy on the regular?" I asked as I squatted a little and pushed inside her.

"As good as you are, I was sure you did it frequently. Oh shit,

Colson. Why can't I get enough of you?" she asked as she wrapped her legs around me.

Lifting her from the countertop and putting her back against the wall, I said, "Because I won't let you. I can't have you being nonchalant about this dick when this pussy got me fiending."

I had my way with her until I'd nutted deep inside of her. When I allowed her to slide from my grasp, I leaned against the wall, wishing I didn't have to leave her today. No words were spoken between us as she went to the vanity to brush her teeth and I went to my duffle bag to retrieve my toothbrush. My phone began ringing, making me deter from my course back to the bathroom. It was Velma... my mother. "Hello?"

"You could have gotten her killed! Why do you insist on being heartless?"

"What?"

"Val is in the hospital! Somebody beat her!"

I closed my eyes for a moment. "Why that shit gotta be my fault? I'm supposed to keep funding her habit? Why can't this be Val's fault for fucking over people? Where is she?"

"She's at Baptist, but I'm sure you won't come anyway. She means nothing to you, and I hate that you can't see past the drugs and remember she's your sister."

She ended the call and I couldn't help but be angry as fuck. I loved my sister, but because I wouldn't fund her drug habit, I was the fucking enemy. I threw my phone to the bed, then snatched my toothbrush and grabbed my shower gel and went to the bathroom as Sky was coming out. Looked like I wouldn't be making it to Houston as early as I intended. Her eyebrows lifted and she asked, "Are you okay?"

"Yeah. We can talk about why you took a mental health day, though, when I come out."

She nodded and I went to the sink and brushed my teeth, then started the shower. My dick was sticky as hell, and my balls were damn near glued to my leg. After getting towels from her linen closet, I got in the shower and let the water spray in my face. Mama was stressing me the fuck out. I couldn't get involved in that street shit no more, but everything in me wanted to go have a talk with Jeremy because I was sure he either fucked my sister up or knew who did. I wanted to be angry at him, but I knew how this shit went. I didn't gender discriminate when a crackhead tried to fuck me over. And I surely didn't accept sexual favors from their dirty asses.

As I was about to wash up, the shower curtain pulled back and Sky got in the shower with me. She took the towel and shower gel from me and began washing my body, causing the tension to leave me. She didn't say a word, but her touch was soothing me in ways that I couldn't soothe myself. My need for her only increased, and I couldn't help but stare into her eyes, giving her me, letting her see my vulnerability, my need for her, and my sadness about my family situation. Staring at her... it was like I could see her soul. God had placed this angel in my path, and I couldn't help but be in awe of her pure spirit. It was like I'd seen God Himself through her at that moment, and I couldn't look away.

She looked away first and continued washing me. Evidently, my gaze overwhelmed her, because a tear slid down her cheek, and I could feel her tremble beneath my hand as it rested on her shoulder. Gently grabbing her chin, I turned her face back to me and softly kissed her lips, allowing my tongue to glide into her mouth. The tremble that went through my body caught me off guard and the heat rushed my face. I slowly pulled away from her as I noticed the goosebumps on my skin. *What was she doing to me?* My anger had dissipated, and all I could feel was the sweet and all-consuming spirit of God.

## ❧ 1 2 ❧

S ky

I COULDN'T STOP THE TEARS THAT TRICKLED DOWN MY CHEEKS
as Colson stared at me. I mean, that shit was penetrating my damn
soul. My heart felt overwhelmed because it felt like he was giving
me all of him already. Although there was so much more we
needed to get to know about one another, it felt like he was giving
me his heart. His face was red, and the goosebumps on his flesh
mirrored mine. It was like we'd experienced something spiritual,
and I couldn't shake it. I continued washing his body, gently
pushing him to turn around. His eyes had never left me until that
moment.

I bit my bottom lip as I washed his back. *How could this man be
pulling all this shit outta me already?* After washing his legs and
standing back up, I wrapped my arms around his waist and kissed
his back. Going from feeling embarrassed to feeling vulnerable in

less than thirty minutes had my emotions topsy-turvy. When he told me what was on my chin, the events of last night played through my head like a damn movie. *A drunk man tells no lies.* I'd heard that statement all my life, and now, I knew exactly what it meant. I was a freak when it came to Colson... wide-open in every way: physically, emotionally, and spiritually. He'd consumed me without really trying, and I believed I'd done that to him as well.

We stood that way for a moment until he turned around and grabbed my towel from the railing and soaped it with my Olay body wash. "So, why did you take a mental health day?"

I felt like I'd told him last night, but it probably wasn't clear since I was drunk. Maybe I thought it. "I had a rough day at work."

"Well, you said that much. But what happened?"

Okay. I did say something to him about it. "The kids were so disrespectful. My earlier classes were fine, but my classes after lunch were pushing me to my limits. I literally wanted to strangle a couple of them. But what really has me bothered is that I'm losing my drive to make a change in these kids. I feel so overwhelmed with trying to teach past the foolishness."

"I understand. We all need a break sometimes."

"I'm sorry about Weslan, too," I said as he washed my legs.

"It's cool. I have a sister... who's now in the hospital for fucking over somebody. According to my mother, they beat the shit out of her and that's somehow my fault."

My eyebrows lifted as he stood. "Wow. I'm so sorry. Are you going to the hospital to see her?"

"Yeah. But back to your issue. Have you considered changing schools?"

"Yeah, but Beaumont United isn't any better. I teach high school, so that means I would have to leave BISD. The other school districts that are close don't pay as much because they're smaller. I can't afford a pay cut. So, I'm somewhat stuck."

"You're never stuck. You'll figure it out. If you need help, I got'chu."

He turned me around and I could feel his growing erection on my back. After washing me thoroughly, I stood under the spray with my eyes closed, enjoying the hot water for a moment until I felt his mouth on my nipple. I opened my eyes and put my hands to his bald head until he lifted it. "Since I'm going see my sister and not heading back as soon as I planned to, I'd like to take you to lunch."

"Okay. Can I go to the hospital with you?"

I felt like he needed me. Just the way he gave me everything inside of him without saying a word told me that. "You wanna come to the hospital with me?"

"I'm your woman, right? I feel like you need me to. I wanna come to be there for you."

"I appreciate that, baby."

We got out of the shower and got dressed. Neither of us seemed to be in a rush, but we weren't playing around much, either. Being around Colson renewed me, and I couldn't let him go to the hospital without me. What would that say about me? After putting my shoes on and grabbing my purse, Colson smiled at me. I'd only moisturized my face and put on lipstick. He gently slid his fingertips down the side of my face and said, "You're a natural beauty. I love that about you."

I smiled at him, and tip toed to kiss his lips. "Thank you, baby."

We headed out to Baptist hospital to see his sister. I was somewhat confused as to what happened to her, so I asked a question for clarification. "So, she got into a fight?"

"Naw. She probably smoked up some shit she wasn't supposed to. My mama said somebody beat the hell out of her. She'd called me and said someone was gonna kill her and she needed money."

My eyebrows lifted. Apparently, he didn't give her the money since she was in the hospital. I could only imagine how he was feeling right now. He glanced at me. "Don't get in your feelings, Sky. She does that all the time to get money out of people. She'd just done it the other day. It's like the little boy that cries wolf. I never give her money because I know the game. All the fiends do it to their loved ones. Mama gives into her, but I never do. I've tried taking her to rehab and she always leaves. I mean... when is enough enough? I feel bad that she's in the hospital, but that shit ain't nobody's fault but hers."

I had no experience whatsoever when it came to dealing with fiends. No one in my immediate family or even cousins that I was close to growing up were that way. So, this was new to me. As we continued our ride to the hospital, my phone started to ring. Nikki's number flashed across and I rolled my eyes. She was a teacher, too, and had probably noticed I wasn't there. I didn't really feel like talking to her. When we'd gotten home Saturday, we'd talked about her behavior, and she swore she was only looking out for me. That I was moving too fast with an older, more experienced man. She was hating, and I was pissed that she would insult my intelligence that way. So, she knew I was pissed at her.

I ignored the call as Colson glanced at me. We were turning into Baptist Hospital's parking lot anyway. I didn't have time to talk. Once Colson parked and we made our way inside, we headed straight to the information desk. After getting her room information, he led me to the elevators. She wasn't in ICU, so that was a good thing. It couldn't have been as bad as he was expecting it to be. I could feel his hand tremble, so I looked up at him and could tell that his teeth were clenched like he was angry. "Colson, you okay?"

"Yeah. I'm good."

I rubbed his hand between mine as we arrived at the fifth floor. Walking down the hallway, Colson seemed like he was on a mission. I didn't know what to expect as he walked into a room without knocking. There was a woman sitting in the bed with her arm in a sling. She smiled, but she looked evil. "Oh, so you do give a fuck."

"Had Mama been truthful and said all you had was a broken arm, I wouldn't have come. She made it seem like you were dying.

When that woman didn't say you were in ICU, I was prepared for the fuckery."

My eyes were wide as his sister introduced herself to me... kind of. "I'm Val. I don't know what'chu see in his old mean ass. You look a lil too bougie for his tastes. He done got out of jail and used drug money to start businesses and think he better than everybody."

"Umm... I'm..."

"You don't owe her ass a response, baby."

"Well, they reset my arm, and I'm getting out of here tomorrow. My blood pressure was high. Otherwise I would have been getting out today." She rolled her eyes at Colson, and then turned her attention back to me. "Don't let Cole tell you what the fuck to do. He good at tryna boss people around."

I was still in shock and really didn't know what to say. She was skinny as hell, but I could clearly see some of Colson's features in her. She was tall, but her skin was somewhat dark. I could tell that had she been healthy, it probably would be lighter. "They need to only release you to rehab. I gotta go. This was a wasted trip. I had shit to do today, and fooling around with you and mama done threw me off schedule. When you get yo' shit together, call me."

"Even if I was in ICU, I don't want you coming to see about me. You don't fucking care about your family. Muthafucka. Get the fuck out my room."

Colson shook his head slowly and pulled me by the hand into the hallway. His skin was so red it was scaring me. He was angry as hell, and I didn't blame him. His sister seemed like she was hard to deal with, and I hoped I never had to see her ass again. When we got to the elevator, Colson remained quiet, so I went to him and wrapped my arms around his waist, laying my head on his chest. He exhaled, and I could feel the tension leaving him as he rested his arms on my shoulders. "Thank you, Sky."

He kissed the top of my head, and then I lifted it to offer him my lips. We kissed once again. When the elevator door opened, there stood the woman I remember from Galveston. *His mother.* She looked surprised to see him, but he looked angry all over again. "Cole, I'm sorry. I just wanted you to come see about her. So, she'd know that you still cared."

He grabbed my hand and led me away from her without a word. Shit, I was glad I didn't grow up with this kind of drama. This shit was tiring and heavy. We seemed to speed walk to the vehicle. Being that his legs were way longer than mine, it felt like I was being dragged. I was practically running to keep up. When he got to the passenger side of his SUV, he stood there facing the vehicle for a moment, and then turned to me. "You mind if we take our food back to your place? I'm not really in the mood to sit in a restaurant."

"No. I don't mind at all," I said softly, sliding my hand to his cheek.

As I caressed it, he closed his eyes and took deep breaths. When he opened them, he stared at me for a moment, similar to the way he stared at me earlier, giving me all types of feels. I was mesmerized and couldn't look away. "You make coming to town worthwhile. I'd deal with all this bullshit if I can come to your open arms, baby."

*God!* It felt like I was gonna cry. He was so passionate, he took my damn breath away when he said things like that. He leaned over and softly kissed my waiting lips, then opened the door for me. If this was what I was missing out on with an older man, then I could kick my own ass for not going there sooner. When Colson got in the driver's seat, he turned to me. "Anything you want in particular?"

I shrugged my shoulders with a smile on my face. *Shit, I wanted him.* "No, so just go with whatever you want and I'll find something."

He frowned slightly. "You sure about that? 'Cause I'll mess around and end up at Popeye's or Sonic, happy and satisfied. So, you better speak now or forever hold your peace."

I giggled. "I'm not picky Colson. If you go fast food, I'm cool with that, too. Sonic has limitless options."

He laughed and I loved the sound of it. Reaching over to grab my hand, he kissed the top of it and shook his head. "Why couldn't I have met you sooner?"

"Because I rarely go anywhere. They practically had to drag me to Galveston. I go to work, an occasional concert and out to dinner with my brother or Nikki. That's it."

"You ever get a chance to talk to Nikki?"

"Yeah. She apologized, but I still haven't felt comfortable talking to her since then. I miss her shenanigans, but I worry whether she's only around me for her own selfish reasons."

"If you love her, give her another shot to get it right. Now if she fucks up again..." He shrugged his shoulders. "Then that's on her."

"Right," I whispered. "We'll see."

"So, THAT'S THE KIND OF NIGGA YOU WANNA BE WITH? ONE that pulls a gun on yo' brother?"

"No. But when you saw his vehicle here, you shouldn't have used your key to come in my house, Weslan. What if you would have walked in on something you didn't wanna see?"

Shit, he almost did. He turned his lip up as he sat on the bar stool. Colson had stayed at my house for a couple of hours after getting lunch from Sonic, and then he headed back to Houston to handle his business. I knew I wouldn't see him tomorrow because I had a meeting. So, who knew when I'd see him again? Maybe the weekend. He'd fucked me like crazy before he left. I was in awe when he lifted me easily against the wall, practically throwing me and catching me with his face. That was some acrobatic shit if I ever saw it. He could always take his aggression out on me if that was how it was gonna be. I was so tired after he left, I took a shower and laid down until my doorbell rang. "You are going to have to give me my space and privacy. I'm a grown woman. I don't need you checking for me like I'm a helpless little girl. Colson is my man now, and I need you to accept that."

He shrugged his shoulders. "I don't have to accept that."

"Why can't you get over his past and accept the fact that he's changed?"

"Because I don't believe the muthafucka has changed. That's what I'm trying to tell you."

"Weslan, I don't wanna argue with you. If that's what you believe, then so be it, but I don't. So, I'm asking that you respect me and Colson and give me my privacy."

"Fine. I'm done with it. Washing my fucking hands. You gon' see."

Just because his ass hadn't changed and was still a weed head, didn't mean that other people couldn't change. I doubt Colson would still be involved in all those other activities and risk his businesses, along with his freedom. I believed Weslan was just jealous that he rose from the dirt and made a name for himself. If he did that with drug money, oh well. I couldn't concern myself with that, because I really didn't care. Weslan stood from his seat. "See you whenever."

"Are you serious? Because I'm not doing what you want me to do, you gon' be standoffish? You smoke weed almost every day and I hate that shit. But I don't tell you that I'll see you whenever because of that. I'm starting to realize that because I've found freedom to be me, the people that took pride in controlling me aren't happy with that. You and Nikki. That's fucking blowing me, Weslan. I never expected that from you. But it is what it is. Get out."

"I didn't mean it like that, Sky. I just meant that whenever I may wanna come over, he may be here."

"I never said you couldn't come over while he was here. I said not to use your key."

"Oh no. I know you didn't say that. But I won't be coming over if he's here."

That wasn't much better. I opened the door for him, and he kissed my cheek and walked out. *Was Colson worth losing my best friend and my brother?* After locking the door, I went back to my room and got in bed and commenced to staring at the ceiling. I couldn't let go of the way Colson had me feeling. I'd never felt this much passion in my life. He seemed a little dangerous, but I liked that about him. He and Weslan had a past, and who knew what all that entailed. It seemed there was more to it with the way Weslan was behaving.

These were times that I wished my mama was here. My eyes watered as I thought about her advice to me some years back. *Baby, if he doesn't make you question where he's been all your life, then he ain't it. The man for you will have you willing to go against the world. He'll make you feel like the queen that you are, and will love without expecting anything but your love in return. When you find him, or when he finds you, don't let him go.*

I smiled to myself as I stared at the ceiling, because she was right. Colson was all that and more. While it was too soon to declare love, we were both smitten with one another. There was no doubt that what we shared could turn into love. Colson was a gentleman and extremely protective. He was everything I desired. While his past wasn't something I would go for, it was just that. His past. Had he been doing those things now, there was no way I would be with him. Colson didn't strike me as a liar.

Grabbing my phone from my nightstand, I typed his name in my web browser. Colson Jermaine Crook. The first thing that popped up was his criminal record. Then there were Smoothie Kings listed and Colson Furniture. I clicked on his criminal history and saw an article about a Port Arthur drug lord being taken down and sentenced to only three years. The public was outraged. There was a picture of Colson in the courtroom with a smug grin on his face. There was that cockiness that I knew he possessed, but it was also a 'you can't fuck with me' type of look.

There was something that was missing from the picture, and

that was his salt and pepper beard. He also had hair on his head. His build was slenderer, and of course his eyes looked younger. That was about the only wrinkles in his face now... the crow's feet at the corners of his eyes. He'd clearly made up for lost time. Since his three years inside, he'd gotten a business degree and perfected his temple. His body was everything women drooled over when they got on Instagram.

Going to his furniture store, I clicked on the link and my mouth fell open. The pieces he had were amazing. But when I clicked on a couch I liked and saw that the shit was five thousand dollars, I knew that site wasn't for me. It was well out of my price range. Just as I sat my phone down on the nightstand, it rang. Bringing it back to me, I saw it was Colson. "Hello?"

"Hey, baby. What'chu doing?"

"Lying in bed, thinking about you."

"Oh yeah? What are you thinking?"

"How much I miss you."

"Uh huh. You don't miss me, you just miss my doggy style."

He laughed, and it was the first awkward moment between us. I had no clue what he was talking about or why it was so funny. I remained quiet until he said, "Aww shit. You don't know Snoop Dogg?"

"Yeah!"

Of course, I knew who Snoop was, but I didn't remember that line. "When Snoop first came out with his first single, at the beginning of the video, this female was saying that she loved him. He was like, *you don't love me. You just love my doggy style.*"

"Oh. That must have been before my time. I probably know the song, but I don't remember ever hearing that line."

"Well, our first moment where our ages come into play. That's okay, baby. I'm gon' hip you to all the old stuff and you can help me get acquainted with all the new stuff."

"I don't listen to all that shit my damn self."

We both laughed and he asked, "Well, do you like Mint Condition?"

"Yeah. I do."

"They will be in Houston in a couple of weeks. You wanna go?"

"I'd love to go. Will it be on a weekend?"

"Naw. A Thursday night."

"Shit. I don't think I can swing a weeknight. I'll be so tired the next day. Those kids will run all over me for sure."

"My bad, baby. I'll keep my eyes open for something to do on the weekends."

"That's okay, baby. So what are your plans for this weekend?"

"Well, there's this fine-ass woman that lives in Beaumont that I plan on seeing. Hopefully she can come to me Friday night and I can take her with me around town to check on my stores Saturday, and then have her all to myself until Sunday evening."

"Is that right?"

"Hell yeah. You know her?"

"I think I might have a clue."

He chuckled and said, "Thank you for being there for me today. Just having you there to soothe me kept me from letting my temper take me places I didn't want to go. I was almost sure Val expected more of a tongue lashing than she got. Your aura soothes me, and I just want you near me all the time. I miss you already."

He made my heart smile. "I want you near me, too. Do you have anything planned for the second weekend in April?"

"Naw. What's up?"

"It's my birthday. I'll be thirty."

"Aww shit. A new decade. We gotta do it big."

"I don't care about doing anything big. I just wanna be with you."

"Well, I plan to spend every weekend from here on out with you, baby girl. I don't ever want you to have a free moment and not be able to see me. Since you don't work weekends, that gotta be time we set aside to spend with one another. So, I'm gonna make plans, but tell me what you like to do."

"I like to read, go to concerts, and skate."

"Really? What about ice skating?"

"Yeah! I haven't gone in a long time, though."

I was so excited to hear someone making plans for my birthday. My past couple of birthdays, I'd gone out to dinner with Weslan and that was it. Nikki always wanted to go to a club to celebrate, but she knew I hated clubs. "When is your actual birthday?"

"April ninth. That Thursday before the second weekend."

"Do you plan to work that Friday?"

"I did, since I didn't have any plans."

"Well, can you take off? That way you can come to me on your actual birthday?"

"Yeah, I'll put in for that day off."

"Okay. Good."

"When is your birthday?"

"June twelfth."

"Okay. I'm saving it in my phone and making a mental note as well. What are you doing?"

"Heading home. I'm almost there."

I closed my eyes, imagining how much I would miss him by the time Friday got here. I'd seen him almost every day for a week. Not one time did I get tired of being around him. His attention was always on me, and I found that refreshing. I hoped we stood the test of time and this thing between us wasn't just seasonal, because my heart wouldn't be able to take it.

## ❧ 13 ❧

C olson

"SO, HAS ANYTHING CHANGED SINCE I SHOWED UP TO THE meeting on Wednesday?"

"Yes sir. Everyone's been showing up on time and seem to be taking me more seriously. I think them knowing that you have my back has a lot to do with it. So, I appreciate you coming."

"Good. If anything changes, let me know, and we'll get some people replaced. Have a good weekend."

"Thank you, sir. You do the same."

I ended the call and headed to my furniture store to check things out. I rarely had to do that. It practically ran itself. The only people that came there were looking to buy something. Most people did their browsing online. The pieces of furniture we offered were high-end, mostly Italian furniture. The elite of Houston and the surrounding areas shopped with us, and I couldn't be prouder at how much it had grown in the past couple of years. While thoughts of expanding weighed on my brain, I settled with leaving things as they were. I had another store in Dallas and that was all I needed.

When I got there, I noticed a couple of people sitting at desks, and a new salesperson walking around the store. I loved to weed out the unqualified. Everyone knew to ignore me when there was a new worker who hadn't met me yet. I winked at Yvonne, my lead salesperson, and went to look at the couches. The new personnel came over to me. "Hello, sir. How are you today?"

"I'm great. Thank you. How are you?"

"I'm excellent. Thanks for asking."

I nodded and continued to look. He watched me closely without saying anything for a little while. "Is there something I could help you with or help you find?"

"I'm looking for the perfect couch to put in my formal sitting area, but none of these seem to be what I'm looking for."

"What is it exactly that you're looking for? Are these in your price range? Because there's actually a furniture store a mile down the road that has much better deals."

I could feel my blood boiling. *Who in the fuck hired this fool?* The new people never expected a black man to own a store like this, so I caught them off-guard every time. "Can I speak to your manager, sir?"

"Umm... sure."

He walked away and went to Yvonne. When he came back with her, I asked, "Is it common practice for the employees to recommend customers to other furniture stores without finding out exactly what the customer is looking for?"

"I'm so sorry, Colson. It is not."

When she called me by name, the salesman looked to have shitted on himself. "You're fired, sir," she said to him.

I shook my head slowly. We had to screen these people better than what we were doing. How many other sales had we lost out on because he'd referred them to another store? When he walked off, I asked Yvonne, "How long has he been working here?"

"A week, but he's only been working independently for two days. I apologize, Mr. Crook. You know he wasn't trained that way."

"Okay. I'm gonna trust you to get better sales personnel in here, Yvonne."

"Yes, sir."

She only called me Colson so the young man would know who I was. All other times, the employees called me Mr. Crook as they should. I walked back to my office and checked our numbers for the month, and we'd done exceptionally well, pushing out right at a million dollars profit. A celebrity or mogul of some type must have come in to furnish their entire house. We saw numbers like that when that happened, which was at least four times a year. As I looked over the numbers, the store manager walked in. "Hello, Mr. Crook. I heard about our mishap with personnel. I do apologize."

"No problem. We just have to figure out a way to better screen people during the employment process."

"Yes, sir. As soon as I come up with something we can implement, I'll let you know."

"Thank you, Lyle. Other than that, everything looks great. I'll be doing evaluations next month, but from what I can see, you all have done well this fiscal year."

"Thank you, Mr. Crook."

I shook his hand, then left out to head to my SUV. He was such a brown nose, but I kept him around because of that fact. He did everything he knew to do to get positive attention from me, which benefitted my business. That was why he got a raise every year. When I got inside, I looked at the time and smiled. It was four o'clock, and my baby should be on her way to me. I couldn't wait to see her. It seemed like weeks and it had only been three days. I'd gotten used to seeing her in just that short amount of time.

Pulling out of the parking lot, I headed to my loft in downtown

Houston at 59 South. I was neighbors to a couple of rappers and a few actors. I didn't see a point in owning a home when it was just me. It gave me time for other things than trying to maintain property. If things progressed as I hoped they would with Sky, then homeownership was something I would give further consideration to. I wanted a family... kids. After getting home and taking the elevator to the top floor, I decided to call Sky to see where she was. We'd been talking every day, and it seemed we'd gotten so close. It hadn't even been two weeks yet, but I already felt like I couldn't live without her. The phone rang until it went to voicemail. "Hey, baby. I was just calling to see where you were or if you'd left home yet. I can't wait to see you."

After opening the door, I dropped my keys on the countertop and proceeded to my bedroom area of the loft. Taking off my clothes, I started the shower, and then grabbed a t-shirt and shorts from the drawer. I thought we could enjoy our night here and tomorrow night I would take her somewhere fancy to eat for dinner. Just as I was about to get in the shower, my phone started ringing. I knew it was probably Sky, so I turned to answer it. "Hello?"

"Hey."

"Hey. What's up?"

She didn't sound like herself... like something was bothering her. "I haven't left yet. I probably won't leave until tomorrow."

"Why? What's going on? Do you want me to come to you?"

"No. You don't have to come to me. I don't feel too good. I think I ate something for lunch that didn't agree with me."

"Baby, I don't mind coming to you."

"No worries, baby. I should be able to come in the morning. I know you have things to do in the morning out there."

*Was she playing me?* Something just didn't seem right. She sounded nervous. "Sky... be real with me. I feel like you playing me right now."

She took a deep breath and said, "I got into a huge argument with Nikki at work. We both got suspended and they are docking my pay. I just wanna strangle her. The two people I was closest to have turned their backs on me since I've been with you. I... I just think that maybe we should cool down a bit."

I could feel my anger rising, but I would be cool about it. "Is that what you really want, Sky? So, you're willing to forget about everything we said we meant to one another?"

"I don't want to forget, Colson. I just want us to slow down... really get to know one another."

Taking a deep breath and exhaling loudly, I responded to her. "Whatever you want. So, you're pretty much telling me that you aren't mine anymore. Am I right in that assumption?"

"Just for now," she said softly.

"Sky, I'm fifty-one years old. I'm not cool with the back and forth. I know what I want, regardless of what anyone else thinks about it. I thought you were the same way, but it's cool. I'll do this your way. I have to go."

I ended the call and got in the shower, not giving her time to accept or reject what I had to say. Love was never meant for me. I'd always been a loner, so I didn't know why I was forcing the issue. Instead of staying in, I decided to go out for a drink or two. After the way we connected, I didn't know how I would make it with less of her. *I wasn't forcing the issue.* It came so naturally. Being with her felt right... everything about it felt right.

When I got out the shower, my phone was ringing, and I saw Sky's number. I couldn't talk to her right now. I needed to calm down. My ego was somewhat bruised. Putting the shorts and t-shirt back in the drawer, I went to my closet to find some navy-blue slacks and a white dress shirt. My phone chimed, alerting me of a text. When I grabbed it, I saw I had three missed calls... all from Sky. The text was from her as well. Pausing for a moment, I debated whether I should even read it. I went ahead and opened it, just to see what she had to say. Not much. *Please forgive me and answer your phone.*

I rolled my eyes, then texted back. *What is there left to say? You've made your decision. I'm going out for a drink. Talk to you later.*

I sat my phone on the dresser and got dressed. Realizing that I would need a few drinks, I called for an Uber. After I'd finished getting dressed, Sky was calling again. She said we needed to cool off, but yet here she was blowing me the fuck up. I decided to answer and give her everything I was feeling, since she seemed to want that. I answered, "What?"

She was quiet for a moment, then she said, "Just because I said we needed to slow down, you don't wanna talk to me anymore? Maybe they were right."

"You said you were no longer mine, Sky. If you are no longer mine, what else do we need to talk about right now? But I mean, since you're allowing other people to determine how you should live your life, there's no telling how this will go. I'm not up for talking to you right now. Frankly, I'm fucking pissed, because I thought we had something special. But again, whatever. I'm not finna just sit on the phone with you. Now, are you done?"

"I guess so. Bye, Colson."

That shit felt final, and it felt like a bullet had pierced my fucking heart. She ended the call as I held the phone to my ear, hoping she would change her mind. Why did she even think I would be okay with phone conversations when I knew what she tasted like? Memories of my cum on her chin flooded my mind, along with me hovered over her, giving her a part of me no one has ever gotten. Shaking my head slowly, I slid my phone in my pocket and looked at myself in the mirror. After rubbing lotion on my hands, I grabbed my keys and headed to the lobby to wait on my ride.

Once I arrived at Brenner's, I sat at the bar and ordered a beer, wishing the night was already over. It was crowded as to be expected on a Friday night. When the bartender brought me out the specialty house draft, I sat there drinking, all in my feelings. I couldn't show that on the outside, though. Looking around, I noticed lots of people were coupled up. That only made me down the beer a lot faster. I wanted to get at Sky's brother, but I knew it was of no use. Of course he wouldn't think I was any good for his sister. But I wondered how she would feel to know that he was purchasing more than weed from me at one time. I wasn't that petty, though. If he could convince her of how she should be living her life, then who was I to beg for her time? She knew what I had to offer her: passion, affection, attention, and eventually, love.

After my fourth beer, I was wondering what I was doing here if Sky was still all I could think about. I called for an uber, and then settled my tab. As I stood to walk towards the door, I felt my phone vibrating in my pocket. Rolling my eyes, I looked at it to see my mother's phone number. The day couldn't get any worse, so I answered. "Hello?"

"Hey, Cole. How are you?"

"I'm good," I said as I stepped outside.

"I wanted to let you know that I love you, son."

"I love you, too, Ma."

"Okay. That's it. I'll call you again soon."

"A'ight."

I ended the call and wondered what was going on that she felt the need to tell me that. It didn't matter. I was gonna go back to doing what I've always done: live life on my terms and handle my business without complicating it with people that were supposed to care.

## ❧ 14 ❧

S<sup>ky</sup>

It had been two weeks since I had a full conversation with Colson. My heart was hurting. While I had pulled away from him, listening to the people around me, Weslan and Nikki were both tripping. She'd confronted me at school two weeks ago to apologize again, and when I asked her if she was jealous of me, the shit hit the fan. I felt so alone. Weslan barely had time for me, and it pissed me off. Everyone seemed to be content with their lives now that I was no longer seeing Colson. It was my birthday, and I was gonna be alone for it. I should have been in Houston, having the time of my life. Instead, I was lying in bed, crying my eyes out.

I let Weslan convince me that Colson had come in and stirred up shit. My life was smooth sailing before he came along. Mama and Daddy were probably turning over in their graves with me dating an ex-con and drug dealer. As I sat in my bed, thinking about how lonely I'd been, I got a text from Weslan. *Happy birthday, sis! Where are we going to dinner at this year?*

*I'm not going anywhere this year. My nerves are bad, I'm tired, and I just want to go to bed.*

I wasn't tired, and I didn't want to go to bed. I wanted the man I'd been calling every day to talk to me for longer than five minutes. He hated me now, and I couldn't blame him. Pushing him away was the wrong decision. Because I had never been to his house, the only way I could go to see him would be to go to one of his businesses and act a fool. I wasn't that chick. My phone chimed again, alerting me of a text. Before I could look at it, it chimed again. When I picked it up, there was a text from Weslan and Colson showing on my lock screen.

My body heated up tremendously, hoping he wanted to talk to me. Saving Colson's for last, I opened Weslan's first. *But it's your birthday! We always go to dinner. Please?*

I didn't bother to respond. Instead, I went to the front and back doors, making sure the chain was on. That way, he couldn't use his key and just come in. I thought about asking him for his key, but instead, I was probably just gonna change the locks. When I got back to my room, I sat on the bed and checked Colson's message. *Happy dirty thirty. Enjoy the turn up.*

My head started to pound from me trying to hold in my emotions. I responded, *Thank you. I'm turning up alone tonight at home. I'm already in bed.*

I was hoping that he chose to continue the conversation. He had to miss me as much as I missed him. After pushing him away, I almost immediately regretted it. I stayed home the whole weekend in my bed. I'd already gained five pounds because if I wasn't at work, I was at home, eating and sleeping. I responded to Weslan, saying, *No. Goodnight.*

I laid in bed, holding my phone to my chest. This wasn't the way I was supposed to bring my thirtieth birthday in. I was off tomorrow with nothing to do. Maybe I could go to the spa and get a massage. As I thought about my day, I got another text. It was from Colson. One simple word. *Why?*

I responded immediately before he got busy doing something else. *Because the person I want to spend it with, doesn't want to talk to me anymore. Even after I've apologized over and over again. What else can I do to let him know how serious I am?*

After a few minutes, there still wasn't a response. I turned on my music and a song called "Untouchable" came on. That did nothing for my raging emotions. I laid there until I'd cried myself to sleep.

My phone ringing woke me out of a deep ass sleep. I wiped the slobber from the side of my mouth. It felt like it was late as hell, but it was only ten. My vision was blurry, but I knew the only person that would be calling me was Weslan. "Hello?"

"Come open the door. Why you got the chain on?"

"Because I'm asleep. Go home."

I ended the call. Then he started yelling through the door. I called him back. "You gon' come open the door?"

"Hell no. Na leave me alone before I call the police! I'm not fucking playing, Weslan."

He finally closed the door and locked it back without a word and ended the call. Whenever I dropped the f bomb on him, he knew how serious I was. After checking my phone to see I still didn't have a message from Colson, I laid back in the bed. Within minutes I'd fallen back to sleep.

DEPRESSION WAS REAL. I OFTEN WONDERED HOW PEOPLE allowed themselves to fall into a depression so deep until they couldn't function. I now knew. I'd spent the entire weekend, wallowing in self-pity and regret. Friday when I woke up, I ate a really good breakfast, but that was the last time I'd eaten, and it was now Sunday. Saturday was a blur. I hadn't left my bed but to use the bathroom. I knew today I had to get myself going. Whether Colson ever talked to me again or not couldn't be a hindrance to me living my life. It was my fault why I'd lost him, and I had to accept that fact and just move on.

Peeling my body from the sheets, I went to the bathroom and started the shower. After brushing my teeth, I got in, letting the hot water renew me. I needed to regain my sense of purpose again, so I knew I needed to find either a different position in the district or change districts altogether. Once I finished, I shaved and handled other hygiene items, then went to the kitchen to find something to eat. Of course there was nothing, so I went back to my room to get my purse. After turning off the lights, I opened the door and ran right into Colson.

My mouth went dry as I stared at him, not knowing what to say, other than, "Hey."

"Hey. Can I take you to lunch for a late birthday celebration?"

"Umm... yeah."

He grabbed my hand and led me to his vehicle. I hadn't said another word, because I didn't want to say the wrong thing. Once I got in, he closed the door and walked around to his side. Felt like my damn heart was in my throat. When he got in, he turned to me and grabbed my hand. "Listen. Before we leave to go to lunch, I need you to tell me what you want. Because if you still on that same shit, I'm done. I can't hang around, waiting for you to get your shit together, Sky. I'm too old for games and that's not fair to me. So, what's up?"

I swallowed hard and looked in his eyes. The same eyes that had me mesmerized from the very beginning were seeking comfort. I could see that he'd been in as much turmoil as I had been. He'd given me so much of himself until he was afraid to trust me with more. The fact that I could see all that let me know just how much he cared for me, because if he didn't want me to see it, then I wouldn't. "I want a relationship with you, Colson. You're the only person in my life that matters right now. I don't care what anyone else thinks anymore. I hate that it took all this for me to see that."

He put his hands to my face and pulled me to him, kissing my lips tenderly, then hungrily. When he moaned in my mouth, I nearly came undone with emotion. Still cupping my cheeks in his hand, he rested his forehead against mine. "Don't make me regret giving you what I've never given another woman."

"What's that?"

"A second chance to play with me."

As he pulled away, I lifted my eyes to his to see just how serious he was. It caused a shiver to go through my body. I'd hurt him. "I'm sorry, Colson. This is just scary. I don't have anybody else. The only two people I thought I had were against us being together. My parents are no longer here, and Weslan has always looked out for me. He just doesn't know when to let go. But I realized the next day, if not the same day, that I wouldn't be able to handle not being with you, no matter what uncertainties I faced. You're the man I want. So please don't make me regret stepping out of my comfort zone and turning my back on everything I've known. I wouldn't be able to handle being hurt by you."

He grabbed me by the chin, tilting my head back. I saw his eyes soften as he stared at me. "I got'chu. You haven't been eating. I can see the darkness around your eyes. So, we'll discuss our relationship a little more when we get back. What do you want to eat?"

I smiled and he rolled his eyes. "We can go sit in a restaurant, Sky. This is your birthday dinner."

"But I would rather start making up for time lost. I wanna lay in your arms and kiss your lips. I missed you. So, Sonic is just fine by me. If we're in this for the long haul, then there will be plenty of time to dine in restaurants."

He shook his head slowly, and for the first time since he'd been here, he smiled. "Sonic it is."

When we got back to my house and had eaten our food, I grabbed the remote to put a movie on. Colson grabbed the remote from my hand and sat it on the table. "Listen, Sky. I need to talk to you, so you know where I'm coming from. This may seem crazy to you at my age, but I've never felt this way for anyone. Because I was in the streets for so long, matters of the heart weren't a first priority, making money was. When I got out of prison, I was trying to make a life for myself outside of my past. I didn't have time to entertain a woman. However, for the past seven years, it seems like I just couldn't find the one that made me truly open up. So, when I finally felt that with you, then you took that away from me, I literally wanted to go find your brother. Real shit."

He slid his hand up my shoulder to my face and rubbed his thumb across my cheek. "Your brother was right about some things, though. I'm dangerous in every sense of the word, but I've learned to check that. Yeah, I've killed people for minor infractions, and things that may seem trivial. But I'm not who I used to be. I haven't had a run-in with the law in almost fifteen years. To say I was in that life for so long, that's impressive. Regardless of what he thinks, when I got locked up, I left that life behind and I never looked back."

I brought my hands to his face and pulled him to me, kissing him with the passion I've had bottled up for the past couple of weeks. He pulled me to him roughly, then pulled my leg across his lap. As I straddled him, he said, "I've worked hard to stay away from that life. That was why I had to move. It was always beckoning me to return. I did use drug money to get started, but I also had investors and people that believed in me to help out. When people can't wrap their minds around how you made it out, they try to pull you back in. I couldn't let your brother try to do that to me. That's another reason why I really had to get away from you. But having you in my life makes me strong enough mentally to be able to handle him."

"Thank you for that. I promise that I won't let him or Nikki sway me when it comes to us and what we have. You're an amazing man, Colson, but tell me... what is it that you see in me?"

"At first, just your beauty and poise. Although we were in a bar, the way you carried yourself spoke volumes to me. Honestly, because of my age, I knew I couldn't pursue something with a woman my age unless one pulled my heart out my damn chest. I want a family... kids to call my own. So, yeah, I was selective. You fit my criteria. But the moment you opened your mouth, you had me. Your voice was like that of an angel. I can't even describe how it happened, but it was like your spirit reached inside of me and pulled mine to it, making love to it. It's powerful. That's why I know if I don't have you, I won't have anybody else."

"Damn, Colson."

I ran my nails down the back of his head and realized that I had what a lot of women dreamed of. I was falling for him, and there was nothing that I would allow to interfere in what we had ever again. Lowering my forehead to his, we sat that way for a while. His arms were around my waist, holding me tightly to him. Finally finding the words, I said, "I'm falling for you, and these past two weeks were torture. And for the record, I've never felt this strongly about anybody, either. Can we pick up where we left off, or do we need to start over?"

He kissed my neck and mumbled, "You see where you're sitting. So, what do you think my answer will be?"

I smiled, then bit my bottom lip as I held his head close to me. "Well, take me to ecstasy and let's live there."

"Gladly. I hope your bags are packed."

Colson lifted my shirt over my head and grabbed my ass, pressing my middle against his, making me wanna just strip down. I didn't need all that foreplay shit right now. I just needed him inside of me ASAP. I believed he had the same idea, because he almost threw me to the sofa and stripped. He yanked my pants off as I assisted him, and then sat back on the couch. Pulling me astride his lap, he pushed inside of me, causing me to moan out my satisfaction. "How dare you take this pussy from me, Sky? You know this shit is mine."

His words alone had her crying out to him, thanking him for returning to her. "I'm sorry, baby. Pleeeease take ownership of your pussy again. Pleeeeease..." I pleaded as he rocked me on his dick.

Dragging his tongue across my nipples had my shit so stimulated I couldn't fathom holding my orgasm. The moment his lips wrapped around one of them, the floodgates opened, and I rained down on him. That only seemed to heighten his desire, because he began thrusting into me slowly, but deeply while he held my hips to him. Laying his head back on my couch, he closed his eyes and bit his bottom lip. That only propelled me forward, wanting to please him beyond what he's ever felt. Leaning over him, I whispered in his ear, "Make love to me, baby."

I gently bit his earlobe and listened to his groans. He was being more vocal than he had before, and I couldn't help but appreciate it. Two weeks wasn't a long time, but going without his stroke for that amount of time felt like an eternity. "Fuck, Sky. I can't make love to you right now. That shit is torture. Let me fuck you."

He gave me a quick thrust that made me scream. His dick had kissed my cervix and pulled her part of the way back with him. My nails had dug into his shoulders as he began slow winding that dick into me. When he gripped my ass, I knew he was about to kill my shit. He didn't disappoint. "Colson! Oh shit!"

"Uh huh. This my shit, Sky? Who the fuck this shit for?"

"Oh fuck! You know this yo' shit. Let me show you."

I lifted my hips, causing his dick to slide out of me and went to my knees in front of him. He stared at me as he licked his lips. Those eyes... my God. They felt like they were penetrating my soul. Lowering my mouth to his dick, he immediately grabbed a handful of my hair, allowing me to tease the head. I deep throated his shit without warning, and his hips lifted from the couch. His grip tightened on my hair as he grunted. "Fuck!"

I put more suction on him, doing my best to summon his nut, and as I felt the head swell, I stopped. Standing swiftly, I mounted him once again and bucked all over his dick. Colson grabbed my breasts, bringing his mouth to one, teasing my nipple. That familiar sensation was making its way down to my kitty and my legs began trembling. Taking a page from my book, Colson flipped me over to the couch. "If I can't get mine yet, neither can you. And a second one at that."

I was panting, needing him back inside of me. Grabbing my hand, he pulled me from the couch and led me to my bedroom. As I walked to the bed, he slapped my ass. "Damn, I missed seeing this shit bounce."

Before I could turn around, he pushed me to the bed and entered me from behind, filling me to the hilt, taking my fucking breath away. My pussy was speaking directly to him, and she was so damned gushy, it was crazy. "Yeeeaaah," he said in a low voice.

"Colson, yes, baby!"

He'd been nutting in me since day one, so there was no way I could stop him now. My orgasm coated his dick right as he shot off in my depths... the depths that hadn't had a birth control barrier around it in a week. But I was so serious about him and what he meant to me, I'd give him whatever he wanted, including a baby. It might have been a crazy decision, but I craved unconditional love as well. A baby could provide what no one else could. But I wanted to think that Colson would always be here for me. And if I got pregnant, I knew he would be as overjoyed as I would be.

## ❄ 15 ❄

C olson

"WHY ARE YOU READY TO MOVE SUDDENLY? I'M NOT understanding. I been trying to get you to move for the last few years. Val done been by there?"

"I'm in the hospital, Cole," my mama cried.

I stared up at the ceiling, inwardly counting, trying to calm my nerves. "What happened, Ma? I'm on my way there, but tell me what's going on."

"Val and some guy came here. She owed him he said. I didn't have any money, though. Val took her anger out on me. She broke a couple of ribs and one of them slightly punctured my lung. They said I'm at a really high risk to get a clot because of my health and age."

"Fuck!" I yelled.

I'd just left a meeting with my marketing team for the furniture stores and had briefly talked to Sky. We'd been back together for a couple of weeks, and things had been going well. She was supposed to be coming to me this weekend, but it looked like I would be heading to Beaumont. Everything in me wanted to go find Val and just send her to her final resting place. "I'm okay, Cole, but like you asked me about a month ago, *When will enough be enough?* I've had enough."

"A'ight, Ma. I gotta stop home to pack some clothes. What hospital are you at? And how long are they expecting to keep you?"

"I'm at St. Elizabeth, and the doctor is saying maybe another couple of days."

"Okay. Did the guy she was with lay hands on you, Ma?"

She got quiet. My temperature spiked, and at that point, I didn't think it was gonna come down. "He just slapped me."

*Yeah, I was gon' have to fuck him up.* "Okay, Ma. Let me call you back."

I ended the call and pounded my fist on the steering wheel. Anger had consumed me, and I knew if I didn't get it off me and quick, I was gonna kill Jeremy. I had to call Sky so she wouldn't come to Houston. On the first ring, she answered, "Hey, baby! You missed me already?"

"I always miss you when you aren't next to me, but that ain't the reason for my call. My mama is in the hospital, so I have to come to Beaumont."

"Oh no! Is she okay? What happened?"

"Val happened," I said, not recognizing my own voice. "My mama is gonna move to Houston with me when she gets discharged."

"Colson? You don't sound good. Can you pick me up before you go to the hospital?"

"Just meet me there."

"No! I said pick me up. You hear me, Colson? Pick me up."

I drug my hand down my face. She was trying to keep me from

doing something I would regret, but she didn't know that I wouldn't regret a thing. "A'ight."

"Colson? Please..."

"I hear you, baby," I said calmer and took a deep breath.

"You can't lose everything you've worked so hard for. Your mom is coming to Houston. She'll be safe after this."

"You right."

"Are you heading to town now?"

"I have to pack a bag, and then I'm coming. Thanks, baby."

"That's what I'm here for."

"Okay. I'll call you back when I hit the road."

When I ended the call, I realized Sky was right. But the main thing that fell on me like a ton of bricks was that had mama not been so damned hardheaded, she would have already been in Houston and this shit wouldn't have ever happened. None of that stopped me from being angry and still wanting to get at Jeremy, but it had taken me off the edge. After I spoke to my personal assistant and let her know what runs I would need her to make, I was arriving at my loft. Once I'd packed about four changes of clothes, I took a quick shower and headed back out.

I couldn't help but think about Val and Jeremy. It was like they were trying to get me back in the game or involved in street shit. Val, maybe not knowingly, but I believed Jeremey had a motive to his madness. Niggas hated to see somebody doing better than them. I had more money than I ever had from hustling. When I got locked up, I was Lo's righthand man. So, I was practically running them streets with him. Jeremy was just a lil runner at the time, trying to progress quicker than he deserved.

When I got locked up, Lo got killed not long after. The shit was shady, but I was only concentrating on getting the fuck out of Port Arthur. That was it. Grabbing my phone, I called my baby to let her know I was on my way to her. The sound of her voice calmed my thoughts about Jeremy. I put on her playlist of Lalah Hathaway, Charlie Wilson, and a few others that would soothe my soul. My playlist would get me in a world of trouble that I wouldn't be able to buy my way out of.

After getting to Sky's house, I grabbed my bag out the trunk and headed to her front door. I realized there was another car in the driveway. I was already feeling on edge. Hopefully, I didn't have to check nobody. Before I could knock, she opened the door with a slight frown on her face. "Hey, baby. Come on in."

I kissed her lips as her brother approached us. He didn't say a word to me, but he looked at Sky for a moment, then leaned in and kissed her cheek. Once she closed the door, I asked, "What's up?"

"He's upset that we're back together and refuses to be here when you are."

"Oh. Perfect. That means I won't have to deal with his attitude. I'm sorry that he's giving you grief, though. I know you love your brother."

"I do love him, but he wants control over me. He's not gonna get it. I... I'm falling for you fast baby, and I can't let him or anyone else stand in the way of that."

I gently rubbed her cheek, and then kissed her again. I was falling for her, too, but for some reason, my mind was working over-time about telling her so. After putting my bag in her room, I came out and we headed to the hospital. Sky held my hand between hers all the way there, and I could see her lips moving a couple times like she was praying. That was the only thing that was gonna totally keep me off Val's ass... prayer.

Once we got there and I'd helped Sky out of the vehicle, we held hands as we walked to the entrance. When I'd spoken to my mama, she informed me that she was on the fifth floor. After getting to her room, I paused. I didn't know what she would look like... what she'd purposely left out. Sky rubbed my back, coaxing me forward. Opening the door, I slowly walked in to find my mother asleep. Her eye was bruised, and she had a couple of other bruises on her face. Taking deep breaths, I walked closer to see her middle wrapped. My anger was growing to an all-time high as I watched her. She seemed to be struggling to breathe a little bit, but I knew it was from the lung puncture. She had oxygen tubes in her nose.

I wanted to wake her up and let her know I had made it, but I also wanted her to get her rest. So, I sat in the recliner and reached out to Sky for her to sit in my lap. She was hesitant, and I could see it in her eyes. Leaning over to me she whispered, "I'm too big to be on top of you in this lil ass recliner."

"Girl, if you don't sit 'cho ass down."

I pulled her by her waist on my lap and reclined in the chair. We fit perfectly fine. "You comfortable?" I asked after kissing her forehead.

"Yeah."

She smiled up at me and rubbed my cheek. As we got extremely comfortable, there was a knock on the door. Sky sat up as it opened. It was a nurse coming in to check Mama's vitals. "Hello. How are y'all."

"Good," we said in unison.

I pat Sky's leg so she could stand and let me up. Walking over to the bed, I tried to keep the anger at bay. "Are you her son?"

"Yes."

"She's been talking about you since we got her situated. She said you own several Smoothie Kings."

"I do. But in Houston mostly."

She nodded as she lifted Mama's arm to check her blood pressure. When her eyes fluttered open and she saw me, she smiled. My anger consumed me at that moment, because she had a tooth missing. My mama was in her late seventies, but she still had all her teeth. So, that muthafucka hit her hard enough to knock a tooth out. I put my fist to my mouth to try to contain my anger. I hadn't even noticed that her lips were swollen until now. The smile dropped from her face as she said, "I'm sorry, Cole. I should've listened to you. This would have never happened."

"Did you press charges?"

"No. I wouldn't say who did this to me."

"Well, I'll be glad to snitch on Val's ass. If she doesn't wanna go to rehab, she can sit her ass in jail."

"You're right, Cole. I've been so stubborn."

She grimaced in pain as she tried to move. I grabbed her hand to try to help her get comfortable, then kissed her head. Closing my eyes, briefly, I opened them to stare at her. "Colson?"

"Yes ma'am?"

"Don't risk your freedom, baby. I can see it in your eyes. I did this to myself by being stubborn and thinking I could help Val. That's my daughter and I love her so much. But I wasn't helping her. I was hindering her and aiding her addiction."

The nurse put the thermometer in her mouth. I glanced back at Sky and motioned for her to join me at my mother's bedside so I could officially introduce them. She stood from her seat as the machine beeped and the nurse took the thermometer from Mama's mouth. "Your blood pressure is a little elevated, but that's to be expected. Do you need something for pain?" the nurse asked her.

"Yes, please."

When the nurse agreed to come back with her Dilaudid and had left, Mama turned her attention to Sky and gave her a soft smile. "Mama, this is Sky, my future."

"Nice to meet you, Sky Crook."

Sky turned all types of red as she smiled and gently shook my mama's hand. "Nice to meet you also."

"When Colson speaks, he means what he says. He's not a joke-ster. So, if he says you're his future, then I know he'll do whatever it takes to secure it and be sure that it comes to pass. Although we've met before, this time is official," Mama said, sounding winded.

"Okay, Mama. Stop talking. You sound winded. Get your rest."

"Okay. I love you, Colson."

"I love you, too."

Before escorting Sky back to our seat, I noticed a detective's business card near her dinner tray. As we sat, I watched Mama closely. She didn't look good. When the nurse came back in, she gave her the pain medication through her IV, then left. The very minute Mama started to doze, I called the detective. "Detective Morgan?"

"I'm calling with information about the assault on Velma Crook. The perpetrators are Valencia Crook and Jeremy Williams."

"And who am I speaking with? How do you know this information?"

"This is her son, Colson Crook. I just got here from Houston. We've been having problems with Valencia for the past few months. She's my sister, but she's on drugs."

"Okay. I understand. Jeremy Williams' name sounds familiar, so I'm almost sure he probably has a warrant."

I listened to him click away, and I imagined he was sitting at his desk. Normally I would have handled this shit myself, but I just wanted to be done with all of it. I wasn't gonna take this shit where Jeremy was trying to take it. He wasn't gonna get the satisfaction of dragging me back to the gutter. He'd better be grateful for these women in my life, because I wouldn't have hesitated to take his ass out.

After wrapping up with the detective and giving him my contact information, I called my assistant to see how things went and she assured me all was well. Once I ended the call, Sky held my face in her hands. "I'm proud of you."

I gave her a one-sided smile and kissed her lips. "Not going after his ass was the hardest shit I ever did. I wanna fuck him up, for real."

"I know, baby. I know."

## ❧ 16 ❧

S ky

WHEN COLSON AND I GOT BACK TO MY HOUSE, THERE WAS A note on my door. I snatched it down, expecting it to be from Weslan, but then I thought about it. His ass would have come inside and left it on the countertop. "Who's the note from?" Colson asked.

I didn't think he saw me snatch it down, but apparently, he did. Looking down at it, I opened it to see it was from Nikki. "It's from Nikki."

"Okay. I'm gonna go get comfortable."

"Okay, baby."

When he walked away, I began reading and the tears came from nowhere. Nikki and I had been friends for a long while, since college, and I missed her. But I couldn't continue having her around me if she was only around me for her own personal gain. I didn't need any toxicity in my life.

*Sky,*

*I am so sorry. My attitude and my disdain towards your new relationship has been uncalled for. We're supposed to be girls and I let you down. I've been so selfish. This shit is so childish and I'm ashamed of myself. When you met Colson and the two of you had spent time together, I got jealous. I could see that you wouldn't have as much time for me. Instead of being happy for you, I was only thinking of myself. You've been waiting for the right man to come and sweep you off your feet. I believe he's the one.*

I had to take a break from reading to wipe the tears from my eyes. I missed Nikki so much. Not having anyone to talk to about my feelings and Weslan's overprotective ass was driving me bat shit crazy. As Colson joined me back in the kitchen, I could see the concern in his eyes when he looked at me. I gave him a tight smile, then continued reading.

*All this time we could've been celebrating your happiness and drinking to the thought of him hooking me up with one of his fine-ass, established friends. I miss you. There's so much more I can say in this letter, but I would prefer you called me. I've been trying to call you for the past week, but I realized that you probably blocked me. I noticed your car was here, so you probably left with Colson. Whenever you have time, please call me. I love you and I promise to do a better job at showing you just how much.*

*Love,*

*Nikki*

After reading her letter, I was still confused. I didn't know how to take her. While we had been friends a long time, I had never been exposed to this side of her. Not knowing whether I should accept her apology and move forward or to ignore it altogether, I just stood there, staring at it. Colson came close to me and gently rubbed my back. "What did it say?"

"The very thing you said. She apologized for being jealous of what we have and being selfish with me. I really don't know how to feel about it, though. What grown woman would act that way towards someone she's supposed to love?"

"You'd be surprised. But you know her better than me. Does she seem sincere?"

"Shit, I don't know. I never would have thought we'd be in the position we're in, so maybe I don't know her like I thought I did."

"Well, think about it for today and decide what you will do tomorrow or the day after. It's all up to you, and being that she was the one that fucked up, everything is on your time. I'm sure she realizes that," he said as his phone rang.

Walking away from him to go get comfortable as well, I could still hear him talking. It sounded like he was talking to the detective. He was giving locations. I knew this was hard for him. Although I wasn't from the streets, I knew that they didn't go to police to handle shit. They handled whatever issues they had themselves. When I went back up front, he was ending the call. Seeing him shirtless always made me warm inside. A fifty-one-year-old that was built like a twenty-five-year-old was unheard of. But here he was in the flesh. Sometimes I forgot he was that much older than me.

I wrapped my arms around him and laid my head on his back. His heart was beating rapidly, so I did my best to soothe him. Rubbing my hands down his tatted chest seemed to do the trick. He slowly turned around in my arms and palmed my cheeks, placing a kiss on my forehead, then my lips. "You're my peace. I don't know how you do that shit, but everything about you soothes me. I'm so glad you're mine again. I can't let you go, Ms. Jones. 'Cause me and Ms. Jones got a thing going on."

I frowned, then realized this was one of those moments where age came into play. "Oh Lawd. You don't know the song, "Me and Mrs. Jones?" You have to know that song, Sky. Or at least heard it once or twice."

I shrugged my shoulders. "That's before my time, baby."

He rolled his eyes and laughed. "Shit, it's almost before my time, but I know it. Come here," he said, pulling me even closer to him. "We gon' have to take a music education and appreciation day soon. You can't be leaving me hanging."

And just like that, the mood was lighter. We were laughing, talking, and kissing, like we didn't have a care in the world. That was what I loved about our relationship. What he didn't realize was that he soothed me, too.

❧

"I'm glad you called for me to come over, Sky."

"I'm still on the fence about this, but I thought maybe we could get some clarification."

Nikki nodded. Colson had gone to see his mother, and I told him that I would meet him there after I talked to Nikki. I'd called her this morning and she came right over. She leaned over to me and grabbed my hand. "I know I owe you more of an explanation, and I've been at war in my mind on just how to tell you this. Remember the guys from the beach that I was flirting with that first day you talked to Colson after the breakfast?"

I frowned slightly. *What did she have to tell me?* "Yeah..."

"The next day when you left with Colson, I hooked up with one of them. We talked, laughed, and then we fucked. The shit wasn't nothing to brag about. The dick was just okay, but I was willing to deal with it, because I liked his personality. He was funny and seemed to be really affectionate. I was hoping I'd found my one... like you had. Well, we had sex again the night before we left, and the other guy from the beach walked in on us. Crazy shit right?"

My eyes shifted, waiting for her to continue with her story. But I noticed, she got quiet and her demeanor had changed. She looked nervous, and the tears were building in her eyes. "I... umm... I didn't know how to tell you, but they raped me."

She burst into tears, and my heart dropped to my feet. As I rubbed her hand, I felt the tears leave my eyes as well. "When he walked in on us, I tried to cover up, but he was like, *Naw shawty, let him see this shit.* I thought they were into some freaky shit, but I let him know that I wasn't with that. When I tried to leave, he threw me to the bed and the other one climbed on top of me. I felt like it was my fault for trusting him. I didn't know his ass from Adam. I wanted to talk to you about it, but you were so wrapped up in Colson, you didn't have time to talk, nor did you notice that anything was wrong with me."

I fell to my knees in front of her and hugged her tightly as she cried. How could I have missed that? Did she hide it that well or did I not pay close enough attention? I hugged her tightly and cried with her. "Nikki, I'm so sorry."

"It's not your fault. You aren't a mind reader. How were you supposed to know anything was wrong? I got angry and jealous that you'd had a great time with your new guy while I was suffering in silence. Calling the police was out of the question, because I didn't want that attention on me. After coming back to Beaumont and we'd fallen out, I felt like shit. Not shining a light on what they did to me only gave them a pass to do that to someone else. I started counseling and filed a police report. I doubt they will find them now, but I filed it anyway. I didn't even know his friend's name."

"God. I wish you would have told me. I'm so sorry that happened to you, Nikki. You know I would've had your back. We would have filed a police report that same day and had a rape kit done on you."

"They wore condoms, so the rape kit would have been in vain." She shook her head slowly, then said, "I'm not using that as an excuse to why I treated you like shit and tried to force you and Colson apart, but I was bitter... upset that you had found what I was seeking. You weren't even looking for him, but he fell in your lap like God dropped his ass from heaven."

She chuckled and I did, too. "Sky, do you forgive me for being a jackass and a horrible friend?"

"I feel like I should be asking you if you forgive me. I wasn't there for you and I made myself unavailable almost from the moment I met Colson. That had to be hard to say to me just now, so I can imagine how hard it was when we were in Galveston. I forgive you, Nikki. Do you forgive me?"

"There's nothing to forgive you for, but so you won't argue about that, yes, I forgive you."

We both stood and hugged one another tightly. Pulling away slightly, I wiped the tears from her face with my thumb and kissed her cheek. I hugged her once again. It felt amazing to have my friend back. As we hugged, her phone chimed. Pulling away from me, she asked, "Can I get a bottle of water?"

"Go ahead. Nothing's changed. Help yourself."

She used to walk up in here like it was her house, too, and I did the same thing when I was at her place. When I saw her taking a pill, I walked closer to her. "What are you taking?"

I realized her phone chiming must have been an alarm, so she didn't forget to take it. "I'm on an antidepressant right now. When I start feeling better, they'll ween me off them."

She looked at the time once again, and said, "I have to go. I have an aerobics class that I'm going to. It helps me work off nervous energy. It's really helping me clear my mind. If it's okay, I'll call you later."

"Of course, it's okay, Nikki! Call me anytime. I love you, girl."

"Love you, too, Sky."

She walked out the house and I was glad I decided to talk to her. I unblocked her number and stared at my phone for a second and smiled. After watching her drive away, I went to the kitchen to get my purse off the countertop, when my phone rang. It was Colson. I answered, "Hey, baby. I'm about to head out now. Nikki just left."

"They had to put her in ICU, Sky. Her lung collapsed."

I could hear the deadliness in his tone. He sounded like he was ready to go find whomever and make them suffer the way his mom was. "Oh no. I'm on my way. Colson, don't leave."

"I'm okay, Sky. I'm not going anywhere. I'm just angry. The police take too fucking long to do their damn job. They have names and addresses. What's the holdup? They should have called a judge to sign off on a warrant and went got their asses last night."

"I know. But don't risk being taken away from me. I know it sounds selfish. That's because it is. I need you."

He was quiet for a moment. Since we'd been back together, I could tell he was holding back somewhat on expressing his feelings. That was okay, though. I'd let him down the first time and I knew he was trying to protect his heart. But this situation with his mother was becoming too much for him. As I walked out the door and locked it, he said, "I need you, too, baby. Hurry up. I'm okay, but I don't know how long I'll be able to say that."

"I'm getting in my car now, baby. What floor is ICU?"

"Second."

His tone hadn't gotten any better. It was getting deeper. If it weren't for this situation, I would think it was sexy. But I knew there was nothing sexy about what he was ready to do. *Did he have a gun? Could a convicted felon own a gun?* "Colson, I need to ask you a question."

"Anything."

"Do you own a gun?"

"Yeah. A couple."

"Are you supposed to?"

"Yeah, I can. I got my rights back about ten years ago. My crime was non-violent, so it was relatively easy to get them back. Where are you now?"

"I'm about five minutes from the hospital on Eleventh Street."

"Hurry, baby."

"I'm going as fast as I safely can. What are they saying about your mom?"

"It doesn't look good. She's on a ventilator, but they don't know if that will help. I'm trying to remain optimistic, but it's hard."

"God, baby. I wouldn't wish that feeling on anyone. I'm almost there."

"Okay. The nurse is calling me. I gotta go."

He ended the call quickly and I hurriedly drove through the light and turned into the hospital parking lot, going straight to valet. I didn't have time to be circling the parking lot looking for a space. After giving them my name and phone number, I practically threw the keys and took off inside the hospital. The elevator seemed to take forever, but when it finally arrived, I pressed the button to close the door right after I selected the floor. I was anxious to get to Colson. I knew what it felt like to lose a mother, but not through ill intentions. Being the man that he was, I knew it was taking everything inside of him to restrain himself from making a trip to Port Arthur.

When I finally got to the waiting area, I didn't see him. I texted him to find out what room in ICU she was in. Shortly after, he appeared behind me and grabbed my hand to lead me to the back. Holding his hand tightly, I could feel the energy surging through him. He hadn't said a word, but when we got to her room, I saw why. They were detaching the ventilator. She was gone. I walked around in front of him and saw the hardened expression on his face. Wrapping my arms around him, I tried to get him to feel something other than the anger that had taken control of him.

His arms were at his sides, and it was like he couldn't acknowledge me at the moment. "Baby, I'm so sorry."

The tears had begun falling down my cheeks as I tried to absorb all his pain and anger. My grip on him got tighter and I held onto him like a shy toddler held onto their mother. Once the medical personnel had walked out, Colson stepped out of my grip like it was nothing and went to his mother's bedside. When I saw the tear leave his eyes, it was impossible to rid my throat of the lump that had formed in it. I cried as I watched him grieve the loss of his mother. Slowly approaching his side, he turned to me and put his arm around my shoulders and kissed my head.

He released me, then leaned over and kissed his mother's forehead. Walking past me, he went to the nurse's station. My phone was ringing, so I took it from my purse to silence it, seeing that it was Weslan. I didn't have time for his shit right now. Looking over at Colson's mother, I noticed that she seemed to have a smile on her face. It was like she was glad to be done with the world and all the mess that came along with it.

As I smiled slightly, I realized Colson hadn't come back in the room. When I looked towards the nurse's station, he was gone. I ran out the room to the nurse's station. "Excuse me, did Colson say where he was going?"

"Umm... Ms. Crook's son? No ma'am. He just said he would be back before the funeral home finished with his mother."

*Shit! Shit! Shit!* The only reason I could think of that would prevent him from telling me where he was going would be because he was going to Port Arthur. My heart sank to my feet as I went back to Ms. Velma's room to wait for the funeral home to arrive. I sat there and tried calling Colson, but to no avail. He wouldn't answer the phone. *God, protect him.* I tried to prepare my heart to lose him. If he got caught, they would put him away for a long time. Because of his past, I understood why he was going after his sister and the guy he'd mentioned. Even without having a past like his, it was a natural reaction for anyone to want to go after the person that took away their loved one.

My hands were trembling, and I was scared out of my mind. Losing Colson was something I realized I couldn't prepare myself for. All I could do was pray that everything would be fine. That somehow, God would intervene and bring Colson back to me.

## ❧ 17 ❧

C olson

THE WOMAN THAT GAVE SO MUCH OF HERSELF FOR ME AND
Val was gone, and somebody was gonna pay for that shit. I'd dipped
on Sky, and I felt bad about that, but not bad enough to go back.
She just had to understand the way my mental was setup. While
I'd become a successful businessman, I was still a hustler and thug
at heart. That was what I grew up being, and those qualities were
instrumental in my success. But right now, those qualities I
possessed were at the forefront of my thinking, and I couldn't seem
to push them out.

I was heading to Port Arthur to find Jeremy and Valencia, and I
wouldn't stop until I did. I knew where every trap house was,
because ain't shit changed since I was running in them streets. I
made it to the first one in fifteen minutes. Pushing my gun in my
waistband, I quickly exited my vehicle and got ready to bum rush

the front door. Pulling my gun from my waistband, I was met with a bunch of crackheads. Maybe they *had* changed. No one was here. So, they'd left this one to the crackheads.

I hopped back in my vehicle and headed to the house where I knew Jeremy frequented. It was where I'd found him and Val a few weeks ago. Checking the time, I realized I'd been gone for almost thirty minutes. Sky had called a few times. I didn't want to hear her disappointment until after I'd done what I needed to do. When I got there, I hopped out again with my gun close to me and headed to the door. I busted inside with my gun drawn and saw Val sitting on the raggedy ass couch. I walked over to her, pointing the gun right at her head. "Get'cho ass up, Val!"

"Cole! Shit! Get that gun away from me!"

I pulled the hammer back, letting her know how serious I was. She stood but fell over. She was so fucking high; she couldn't even maintain her balance. Leaving her there, I went traipsing through the house to see if I could find that nigga. He wasn't here. Lucky for him. When I went back up front, I grabbed Val by her hair and started dragging her ass while she screamed. My face was twitching, and my lips were tight. Everything in me wanted to make Val hurt for what she'd done and allowed to be done to our mama.

When I got to the car, I threw her ninety-pound ass in the backseat. She couldn't weigh more than that, because she looked skeletal. Drugs had eaten her up from the inside out. She tried fighting me to get out until I held the barrel of the gun against her forehead. "Cole! You would kill your own sister?"

"Without a doubt. Drugs done took you most of the way already. Now jump at me again and I'm gon' send your murdering ass straight to hell."

"I ain't murder nobody!"

"Our mama died today while you were in this fucking house getting loaded. You know how she died? Huh!"

"Mama died? Who am I gonna go to?" she cried.

"You broke two of her ribs, and one of them punctured her

lung. Her lungs collapsed and it killed her. You did that shit! Now sit'cho ass here."

I slammed the door on her while she screamed and cried. She wasn't trying to get away now. She was in shock because her safety net was gone. It was a shame that a fifty-five-year-old woman still had nothing. Had lived life on her own terms all her life. When her husband left her, she went downhill, not being able to cope with his betrayal and had turned to drugs. That was years ago. Despite how much help I tried to give her, she refused it. I drove to the last house I would visit for the day, because I needed to get back to the hospital. "Stay yo' ass in here." I said to Val.

When I got out, I noticed a car in the driveway, so there were probably more people in there than I wanted to deal with. Tucking my gun in my waistband, I knocked on the door and nothing happened. So, I pushed it open to find the front room empty. That shit was highly unusual for a trap or crack house. Pulling my gun from my waistband, I headed to the hallway to check the rooms. Someone was here. As I walked down the hallway, a man stepped from one of the rooms with a gun in his hand. He was trembling and sweating. When he noticed me, he lifted the gun and we stared at one another. It was Weslan, Sky's brother. "What the fuck you doing here?"

"I could ask you the same question," he said, staring at me.

I lowered my gun and he did the same. "I'm looking for Jeremy."

"He got a hot one in him already."

"He's responsible for my mother's death. She died today."

"Well, he succeeded in bringing you back to the gutter. That was his plan all along. Let's get out of here and I'll explain."

"Meet me at St. Elizabeth. I gotta get back."

"Is Sky there?"

"Yeah."

"Get my number from her. I don't wanna talk in front of her."

I nodded then left. *What in the hell had happened?* Whatever the reason was that Weslan took Jeremy's punk-ass out, I was grate-ful. My hands didn't have to get dirty. When I got back to the SUV, I thought Val had left, but when I opened the door, she was laying on my backseat crying. I almost felt sorry for her, but then I remem-bered she was the reason Mama was gone. Putting the truck in gear, I peeled off, heading back to the hospital to face Sky.

When we got there, I drug Val out the backseat. I wanted her to see what she'd done. Several times, I wanted to pull over and put her ass out. When we walked inside, she ran to the bathroom. She probably had to throw up. I wanted to throw up all the way here, because she stank like hell. The police were probably looking for her ass and she was gon' be charged with murder now. When she came out, it looked like she'd tried to wash her face, and she'd wet her hair and tried to pull it back in the rubber band it was tangled around before she went in. I pressed the button for the elevator, and then we went to the second floor. When we got off the elevator, I rang the bell at the door for ICU. It wasn't visitation time, so the doors were locked. After I told them why I was there, they disen-gaged the locks and I walked in. Sky was standing in the hallway with her hands together like she was praying.

As we got closer, she lifted her head and ran to me, hugging me tightly. She released me as I realized the funeral home was still in there, getting mama in that black bag. Val ran in there and was screaming and crying. I rolled my eyes and didn't try to console her at all. Sky was staring at me, and I could see the questions in her eyes. She lowered her head, then looked back up at me. "Was she the only reason you left? I mean... did you leave just to go find her?"

When I didn't answer her, she lowered her head again and wiped her hand down her face. She already knew the answer to that before she asked the question. If I only left to find Val, I would've told her I was leaving. But I didn't want to lie to her, so I left while she was distracted. "Thank you for staying," I said, lifting her head by putting my fingers under her chin.

"Did you?" she asked.

I knew she needed to know if I'd killed him. Thinking about Weslan and what he'd done, I needed to know why. *Was that nigga on that shit?* "Naw. I didn't. It wasn't because I wasn't looking for him, either. Had I found him, he would no longer be in existence. I'm sorry, but it was hell on me just sitting still, not trying to find his ass. Please understand, baby."

I held her face in my hands as I stroked her cheeks with my thumbs. She nodded but didn't say anything else. As she slid her trembling hand in mine, I didn't know what to make of it. She could have chosen to walk out on me, but she didn't. But she wasn't saying anything, either. It could have been that she just didn't want to talk about it now. Val was still in there screaming, so I let go of Sky's hand and went inside the room. I yanked her away from our mom's body so the funeral directors could finish and said roughly to her, "Shut the fuck up. This is your fault. I ought to call the cops and let them know I have yo' ass. You wasn't doing all that crying when you were fighting her and broke her ribs. Then you left her like that. She could have died in the house alone. Now, shut up before I shut you up myself."

Val wiped her tears and struggled to stand there somewhat emotionless as the funeral directors got particulars from me about what we wanted and my contact information. Then, we watched them wheel my mama out of the hospital in that horrible black bag.

"WHAT WOULD I HAVE DONE HAD YOU FOUND HIM, KILLED him, and got caught? Was it worth the risk? Would that have brought your mother back?"

I sat on Sky's couch, watching her pace back and forth. She was upset, but I couldn't apologize for a thing I did. If I had a chance to do it over, I would have gone after his ass sooner. When we left the hospital, I dropped Val off back where I found her. There was no way I would bring her to Sky's house. If she wanted, I could have brought her to a hotel room, but I believed I brought her right where she wanted to be. She didn't protest one bit. When I got here a few minutes ago, Sky went right in. "Baby, I'm trying to understand. I really am. But it's hard for me. I didn't grow up believing that you just took the law in your own hands. Our tax dollars pay for assistance from the police force."

She swiped her hand down her face as I reclined on her couch with my legs stretched out. I wasn't in the least bit stressed. It actually felt good and was an adrenaline rush to even think about fucking Jeremy up. I guess if I told her that her brother killed him, she would pass out. He was raised by the same two parents as she, but he obviously learned a different lesson, whether it was from their parents or an outside influence. Sky walked to the kitchen and yelled back, "You want a drink? Some Henny?"

"Yeah. Please."

I pinched the bridge of my nose. I hated arguing, although we weren't really arguing. Nothing had come out of my mouth since we got here. Trying not to think about Val and my mama was taking the lil bit of energy I had left inside of me. My grieving process had been replaced by anger, and I would much rather be angry than to be crying or all in my feelings. The arguments she and I had about Val came to my mind anyway, though. I wished we wouldn't have wasted time with arguing because we both knew she wasn't going to stop seeing about Val. Sky came back with my drink, handed it to me, then plopped down next to me.

I swallowed it all in one gulp, then pulled out my cell phone to make some calls. After calling my assistant, she promised to send out memos to direct all questions to her email address. Once that was all squared away, I turned to her and just stared as she nursed on her drink. When she sat it on the coffee table, she turned to me. I was waiting to hear what she had to say, because I could see it in her eyes. "I'm sorry if it seems I can't grasp the way you handle things. I'm just afraid of losing you, Colson. I love you and I don't wanna be without you... ever."

My eyebrows went up slightly. *She said she loved me.* Gently pulling her to me, I kissed her lips. "It's okay, Sky. I'm here. I have way too many emotions going through me right now. When I tell you I love you, I wanna be absolutely sure about what I'm feeling."

I stroked her cheek, and I knew she wanted to hear me say it back, but I just couldn't right now. "I care so much about you. I just need some time. Okay?"

She nodded and leaned against me. Holding her in my arms was what I needed right now. I needed someone to be willing to let me take care of them. It was how I showed my love to the ones I loved. Mama and Val had both rejected my love. I felt like I loved Sky, but I had to be absolutely sure. I kissed her head a couple of times, and then rested my head on top of hers. "Colson?"

"Yeah, baby?"

"As I sit here thinking, I can't hold what you did against you. Any man in your position would be ready to kill someone to avenge their mother's death. I'm sorry for being scared and selfish."

"We good, baby. I'm not upset with you. I'm actually thankful for you. You're showing me how much you love me. While you may have disagreed with how I went about things, you didn't leave. You stayed at the hospital and waited for the funeral home. I appreciate that more than you know. I promise to make it up to you."

"There's nothing for you to make up. I told you I love you. I'm here for whatever you need from me. I know what this loss feels like. You can be open with me and trust me with your heart, vulnerabilities, and hurt. Even in your anger, I got'chu, babe."

"Damn, girl."

Pulling her in my lap, I wrapped my arms around her waist and let my hands rest on her ass, then laid my head on her chest. She rested her arms on my shoulders and kissed my head. "Why don't we go lay down, baby? It's been a long day."

"Yeah. I saw your brother on my way back to the hospital and he asked me to call him. He was pretty decent with me, so can you give me his number?"

That wasn't an entire lie. I did see him when I was on my way back to the hospital. This untruth was warranted, though. If he wanted her to know what he'd done, he could tell her. Although, I could be petty with as much grief as he gave Sky about dating me, that wasn't my style. He'd done me a favor by taking Jeremy's grimy ass out of here. Sky frowned. She was too smart for her own good. I knew I should have told him to ask her for my number. "Where did you see him? Was he in Port Arthur?"

"Yeah."

"I knew he still smoked weed. He tried to lie to me and tell me he quit. I could have sworn I smelled it on him the other day."

I wanted to take a deep breath and exhale, thanking God she didn't read more into it than what I wanted her to. I handed her my phone and she programmed his number in it. Afterwards, she leaned over and kissed me. "I swear I'm not myself when I'm with you. It's like I'm somebody else. But now you're starting to see all of me, and that's hard for me to handle. I don't want you to think you made a mistake by loving me."

"I could never think that. My soul... my spirit doesn't lie. They're both excited whenever I'm around you or just hear your voice. That feeling is amazing."

I kissed her again and allowed her to stand so I could get up. She was right. It had been a long day and I was tired as hell. Drained. I stood and followed her to the bed. I'd call Weslan tomorrow.

## ❧ 18 ❧

S ky

"I'M SORRY, MAMA. THAT WAS BULLSHIT. I GOT CAUGHT UP ON some stupid shit," Colson mumbled.

I didn't know how he was getting any rest. He'd been talking in his sleep for the past hour. I'd sat up and rubbed his shoulders, laid on top of him, and held him. Nothing seemed to soothe his soul. He was hurting, but he refused to show it while he was awake. I could hear it in his voice while he was asleep, though. I got up from bed and went to use the bathroom, and when I came back, Colson was sitting on side of the bed. "You okay, baby?"

"Naw, not really."

He stood and went to the bathroom while I sat up and waited. I hated to see him in so much pain. The anger had dissipated, and he didn't know what to do to hide his emotions. When he came out, I stood from the bed and stopped him as he tried to lie back down. "Colson, I got'chu, baby. What do you need?"

He stared in my eyes and gently stroked my cheek, then pulled my shirt over my head. As he teased my nipples with one hand, his other hand slid into my shorts. "Can I have some of this gushy shit?"

"You don't have to ask for that, Colson. You're free to my body anytime you want it."

"Mmm. I more than want it right now. I need it."

"Well, lay down and I'll make sure to give you the ride of your life."

"Shit. You don't have to tell me twice, baby."

He pulled off his underwear with the quickness, and I took off my shorts and underwear. I went to the bed and immediately straddled him. Lifting my hips, I slid down on him, causing him to groan. As I began my ride, I slid my hands up his abs to his chest, teasing his nipples. I wound my hips on him as he held me at my waist. "Shit, Sky. That shit feels good, baby."

Pulling my feet straight out in front of me, but still straddling him, I began rocking on his shit, letting his dick perform a relaxation massage on my cervix. That shit felt so good. It was like he hit every erogenous zone on my body at once, and I was the one doing all the work. My legs trembled as I came, allowing my eyes to roll to the back of my head. As soon as the wave had subsided, I sat up, feet flat on the bed and began bouncing on his shit as he held onto me by my hips. I was a big girl, but I could hang with the best of them.

Listening to his grunts and groans as I pleased him, I couldn't help but feel the love he had for me, even though he wouldn't say it. This was a hard day for him, and I knew it would be hard for him for a while. But he didn't have to say he loved me for me to feel it. The way he reacted when I pulled away from him weeks ago told me that he loved me and everything about me. The fact that he even came back to me after that spoke volumes to me. "Ahh shit, Sky!"

I could see his muscle definition in his arms, shoulders and chest as he tried to hold that nut off, but I was doing my best to pull that shit right out of him. "Quit holding it, baby, and give me that shit," I said through my pants.

When I squeezed my walls around him, he didn't have a choice but give it up. He slammed me down on his dick as he partially sat up and yelled, "Fuck!"

We sat that way for a minute or so, then he collapsed back to the bed. Easing off his dick, I went to the bathroom to get a towel to clean us up. After cleaning myself, I went back to the room to clean him up. He'd already fallen back to sleep. Smiling softly, I gently cleaned him up, doing my best not to wake him up. I threw the towel in the hamper, then came back to the bed and laid next to him, going straight to sleep.

I GOT UP EARLY, BECAUSE I KNEW COLSON PROBABLY HAD A lot to do today. He needed a decent breakfast to help get him through the day. I didn't bother getting dressed. After throwing on a robe, I went to the kitchen to make pancakes, eggs, and bacon. Colson was a heavy eater, so I was sure to cook quite a bit. Before I could finish the eggs, he walked in the kitchen with a smile on his face. "Damn, baby. You knocked my ass out last night and now you cooking breakfast. Shit. I couldn't ask for a better woman. Thank you," he said as he sat at the bar stool, watching my every move.

"It's the least I could do, Colson. What's on your agenda today?"

"I have to go to the funeral home to make arrangements and pay for everything, and I have to find Val again and let her know when everything will be. Then, I'll call your brother."

"You want me to come with you?"

"Only if you want to, baby. But I'll be good by myself. Can I put a request in for dinner?"

"Of course. Whatever you want."

"Can we have chicken fried steak and mashed potatoes?"

"Of course. I'll just have to go to the store. You sure you'll be okay alone?"

"Yeah, babe. I appreciate you."

"Okay. Well, after you leave, I'll head to the store," I said as I sat his plate in front of him.

He closed his eyes and took in a deep breath with a smile on his face. "Damn. You tryna spoil me?"

"Yep. Then you won't ever wanna be without me."

"You *think* you want that, but I can be quite demanding if I'm spoiled."

"Well, what would one of your demands be?"

"That you move to H-Town."

He said that shit without thought. It made sense that he would want me closer to him, and I could teach anywhere. Most of his businesses were in Houston or close in proximity. "That's it?"

"That you let me take care of you."

"Take care of me how? You already do that."

"I mean in every way... spiritually, emotionally, physically, mentally, and financially."

I frowned slightly. "But I work. I can take care of myself financially."

"I'm sure you can, but not like I can. I don't have a problem with you working if that's what you're thinking. But your check can be for your enjoyment. You shouldn't have to be worried with bills and shit."

*Well, got damn.* He was a manly man. I mean, he knew what it meant to put his queen on a damned pedestal. Old school. I smiled at him and brought my plate to sit next to him, along with a couple bottles of water. After sitting that down, I got our coffee from the

Keurig. When I sat, he grabbed my hand and blessed the food. We dug in and Colson moaned. "These pancakes are the bomb."

"Thank you."

As we ate, Colson asked, "So what do you think about what I said? You think you could handle all that?"

"Yeah, when the time is right."

"Good. Because I'm sure the right time is coming sooner than you think."

My eyes widened slightly. *Was he gonna tell me he loved me?* That was the only way I would take such drastic measures. He'd have to completely open up to me before I moved to Houston. I nodded as he watched me from the corner of his eye. My body trembled slightly under his gaze. The things he did to me just from staring at me were indescribable. Once we finished eating, Colson went to take a shower while I made a grocery list. As I did, Nikki sent a text. *Hey! What are you doing today? Are you busy?*

I smiled, then responded, *I will be here all day. Colson's mother passed away yesterday. He'll be gone for a few hours, so I'll be here cooking dinner. You coming over?*

*Yes. I'll be there in a couple of hours. That cool?*

*Yeah. I should be back from the store by then. See you soon.*

I continued making my list in the notes app on my phone, then went to the back to take a shower as well. When Colson stepped out of the bathroom, I couldn't help but look down at that snake hanging between his legs. He was so fucking fine. If social media caught wind of this fifty-one-year-old sex symbol, he wouldn't be able to step out in public again. Not only was his physique amazing, but his sex drive was just what I needed. He didn't usually nut more than three times, but the sessions lasted a while, except when I was slurping that shit up. I licked my lips as it started to rise. "Don't worry. I'll give you all you can handle tonight."

"Shit, you promise?"

He chuckled as he got dressed. I couldn't take my eyes off his dick until he covered it. And even then, I was stealing glances at the print in his drawers. "Nikki is coming over."

"Oh yeah? I'm glad y'all were able to talk things out."

"Me too."

I dropped my robe as he watched me and went started the shower. When I came back and walked past him, he slapped my ass. "Hell yeah. I'm going mining tonight."

I giggled as I got clothes out to wear to the store. Colson kissed my neck, then my lips and said, "I already can't wait to get back and I ain't even left yet."

I pulled his face to mine and kissed him passionately while he squeezed my ass. He quickly pulled away and said, "Man, listen. You can make me forget about all kinds of important shit. Let me get out of here, so I can get back."

I giggled. "Okay, babe. I love you."

He smiled, displaying those beautiful white teeth, then walked out the house. After locking the door behind him, I went back to the shower. How was Colson so damn perfect? Physically, he looked like he was the black King Triton or some shit. He was so damn fine. I had so many imperfections. I was comfortable with my imperfections, but it was hard to believe that he was comfortable with them, too. I wasn't a size six. I was a voluptuous size sixteen without a waist trainer. One of my titties was bigger than the other one, and my birthmark discolored my leg.

As perfect as he was, he didn't seem to have a problem with any of that. That alone made me fall for him even more quickly. His business swag was everything, but when I got a glimpse of that street in him, it was more appealing than I cared to admit to anyone. Learning about his past was tough, but the fact that I was willing to stay and get to know who he was today, told me just how special and rare he was. That Galveston trip was definitely worth it.

After I finished my shower and had gone to the store, I began prepping for dinner. I'd gone to Sonic and got a shake and some cheese sticks to calm my stomach, then got right to work. I'd seasoned the cubed steak and peeled the potatoes. I also bought green beans and cornbread mix. He was gonna be sucking his fingers clean after this meal. When I'd finished, the doorbell was ringing. I knew that was Nikki. When I opened it, she was standing there, looking nervous. "Hey! What's up? Come on in."

"Hey, Sky. You started cooking?"

"Not yet. I just finished prepping. You okay? You look nervous."

I walked to the kitchen and she sat at a bar stool, twiddling her thumbs. "I'm okay. But I *am* nervous about what I want to talk to you about."

That prompted me to stop what I was doing and turn back to her. She was serious as hell. *Why didn't she tell me all this shit at once, instead of spreading it out?* I wanted to roll my eyes, but I was somehow able to contain myself. Walking over to her, my security wall went up... the one I'd gotten used to having with her and Weslan. After sitting next to her, I asked, "What's up?"

"Weslan and I have gotten close."

I sat there, quietly waiting for her to continue. What was so bad about that? I could care less that she was thinking about talking to my brother. Maybe he could stay out of my business since he had some of his own. "We've been seeing one another since before the Galveston trip."

*Shit, wait a minute.* Why was she fucking somebody else if she was talking to Weslan? "What? Why are you just now telling me?"

"I don't know. I thought you would be upset. Y'all are so close. But I needed to tell you, because we've gotten serious about us now. For the past couple of weeks actually."

*Oh. They weren't serious yet.* She had me jumping to all sorts of conclusions. "That's cool. So, you tryna be my sister?" I asked, then let out a chuckle.

She chuckled, too, but added, "There's more, Sky."

The smile fell from my lips as I stared at her. "I told him about what happened in Galveston when he questioned why I was on antidepressants. He threatened to leave me if I didn't tell him the guy's name. When I did, he described someone he knew by the same name, and it happened to be the same person. I haven't been able to get ahold of him since yesterday. I'm scared he may have gotten in trouble, Sky."

"Shit. What was the guy's name?"

"Jeremy."

I frowned. Colson had mentioned that name when he was talking to the police. *What in the hell was going on?* "Is he from Port Arthur?"

"Yeah."

"Shit. I think that's the same guy that assaulted Colson's mother before she ended up at the hospital. He was looking for him, too."

I grabbed her hand, my mind running through all the possibilities. Weslan wasn't a violent person. Him trying to find her assailants just didn't seem like him. And once he found them, what would he do after that? Get killed? That shit had my nerves on ten. Standing from my seat, I paced back and forth, then grabbed my phone and called him. He didn't answer. I then called Colson to see if he'd gotten in touch with him, but he didn't answer, either.

"Shit! What if they hooked up and went to find him together?"

I felt like I couldn't breathe as I walked to the couch. Deciding to text Colson instead, I sent, *Baby, please call me. It's important.*

Nikki came and sat next to me and grabbed my hand. I felt like praying. *Would I still want to be with Colson if he killed that nigga?* Hell yeah. I just didn't want to lose him. What was the likelihood that he would get away with it? I mean, he'd killed before and got away with it, but that didn't mean that would be the case this time. As my thoughts ran wild like the stampede on the Lion King, my phone chimed, scaring the fuck out of me. Before I could see what the message said, the phone rang. Colson... Lord, thank you. "Hello?"

"Baby, what's wrong?"

"Did you get in touch with my brother?"

"Yeah. We're meeting after I find Val."

"Okay. He wasn't answering his phone and it scared me."

"You sure you okay?"

"Yeah. I'm sitting here with Nikki, now."

"Oh. Okay. Well I'll call you when I'm on my way back, baby."

"Okay. I love you."

I ended the call, since I knew he wouldn't say it back. No sense in listening to his silence. Nikki was staring at me, eyes wide. "He talked to Weslan briefly, but they hadn't had their sit-down talk yet."

"You love him?"

The heat rushed to my face. "Yeah. He's everything I want, and he's fine as hell. It was easy to fall in love with him."

"What about him?"

"He hasn't said it yet, but everything he does to me and for me says that he does. I just told him for the first time yesterday."

"Wow. I'm surprised you told him."

"Me too, but I couldn't hold it in any longer." I sat quietly for a moment, thinking about how much I loved Colson, then shifted my thoughts back to Weslan. "Umm... back to Weslan. Maybe he doesn't want to talk to us because of what he's trying to do."

"Maybe," Nikki said softly.

Looking at my phone, I remembered I'd gotten a text. When I accessed my messages, I saw it was from Weslan. *Hey sis. I'll be over later. I'm busy right now. Tell Nikki to stay there and I'll talk to her then.*

"Weslan said to stay here until he gets here."

"Okay."

We sat there holding hands, trying to figure out what was going on, both staring into space. Whatever was going on, we'd know soon enough. As long as they were both okay. That was all I could focus on right now. Standing from my seat, I went to the kitchen and put a pot of water on the stove to boil the potatoes. We'd have to deal with their shenanigans soon enough, so I cranked up the music on my phone as Nikki joined me. "So, how did you and Weslan start talking? Y'all have always been friends, but when did it turn into more?"

"About two weeks before Spring Break, I saw him in the grocery store. We walked and talked the entire time I was shopping. After he helped me load my groceries, he asked me why the conversation had to end. The way he looked at me let me know how serious he was. I told him to call me and that was it."

"Well, damn. Look at y'all. I hope it works out for y'all."

"I think it will. It wasn't like we had to get to know one another. He possesses a lot of the qualities I love in a man and vice versa. So, we've progressed quickly. He asked me to be his and I said yeah."

I smiled at her and just how happy she seemed when she talked about Weslan. Talking about Colson brought those same emotions out of me. Hopefully, both our men maintained their freedom, because I didn't have a good feeling about them meeting up.

## ❧ 19 ❧

C olson

"She on Thomas Boulevard."

"How you know?"

"I'll tell you when we meet."

"If you say so."

I ended the call with Weslan and headed to the house on Thomas Boulevard. He'd called to see if I was done handling my business so we could meet. I hadn't found Val's high ass, and I'd been to three houses that I remembered. The one on Thomas Boulevard had slipped from my memory. I had a funny feeling that Sky didn't know her brother as well as she thought she did. For him to know where Val was, he wasn't just a client. He was the fucking president! I was willing to bet that he was close to the top of this drug game out here, and now that Jeremy was gone, he probably *was* the top dawg. Ain't *that* some shit.

When I got to the house on Thomas and had gotten out the car, niggas was all in my shit, trying to see who I was. They were a bunch of young niggas, so I didn't know who they were. As I walked closer, one of them said, "Oh, that's OG, right there."

I frowned. I didn't know how he knew who the fuck I was, but I didn't give a damn. As long as I didn't have any problems, I was cool. When I got closer, he held his hand up to slap mine. "You looking for Val, right?"

"Yeah. She in there?"

"Yeah. She was on the couch when I left out."

I gave him a head nod and walked inside. Weslan had told him I was coming, which let me know that my assumption about him was right. *He had the juice.* I chuckled inwardly at the thought and looked around for Val. She was no longer on the couch. Walking further into the house, I looked in the kitchen, then went down a short hallway. And there she was, in a back bedroom. I wanted throw up every got damn where as I watched my sister give this young nigga head. "Val!"

She jumped and fell backwards, looking up at me with fear in her eyes. Lil nigga said, "Yo, wait yo' turn, nigga."

"How much she owe you?"

"Man..."

I pulled my gun and pointed it in his face. "I asked how much she owe you?"

"Twenty-five dollars."

I threw forty dollars at him, then yanked her up from the floor and halfway drug her out the house. When I got outside, that lil nigga she was sucking off had come out the house and put a gun to the back of my head. Young niggas had bitch in their blood. I knew that because he let me turn my back and walk out with Val before he tried to sneak me. "Who the fuck you think you is, nigga?"

"A nigga that will tell you that you better shoot me, because if you don't, you may not live to tell anybody about the day you pulled a gun on Colson Crook."

I heard him suck in air as that other young buck came running up. "Nigga, why the fuck you pulled a gun on Crook? You got balls, nigga!"

"'Cause his pride was hurt. Felt like he got punked. Now what the fuck you gon' do?" I asked in a low voice.

I could feel Val trembling in my grasp as Weslan pulled up. I turned around to face that nigga as he dropped his gun. The minute he did, I pulled my gun and knocked him out with it. Stupid ass. "Yo, don't be coming here knocking niggas out," Weslan said, then held his hand out to me to shake.

"Yo' sister gon' be mad as shit."

"No she ain't, because she won't know."

I shook my head and brought Val to the passenger side of my vehicle. "Get in. We need to talk."

She nodded. After closing her door, I looked at Weslan and shook my head slowly, still trying to process this shit. "Give me about ten or fifteen minutes."

"A'ight. I'll meet you at Judice's."

I nodded, then got in the car with Val. She looked scared, but I was only gonna give her one more chance to leave this life behind. If she didn't take it, shame on her. "So, the funeral is gonna be in three days. There was no point in holding Mama body forever. We're her only two kids, and her only sibling died a while ago. Ain't none of the family ever visited her, so fuck them. I'm just tryna get this over with. Now, if you want, I can put you in a hotel room in Beaumont until the funeral. We can go shopping for you something to wear tomorrow. But no drugs. No runs. After the funeral, I'll check you into a rehab and you can start getting clean. Do that for Mama. I won't turn you in. You obviously don't have a record, or they would have your ass by now."

She started crying and dropped her face to her hands. I took that as a good sign. Pulling her hand from her face, she said, "I thought after what happened to Mama you were really done with me, Cole. I'm tired of being this way, but I know I can't do it by myself. Knowing what I did, I didn't want to be sober to feel it. But what I realized was that I can't do enough drugs to forget. I killed my mamaaaaa," she said, then sobbed.

She made a damn tear leave my eye. I quickly wiped it. "So, look. I gotta meet with Weslan before we leave Port Arthur. I'm gonna bring you to Mama's house to get you some things packed. When I come back, be ready to go. Okay?"

"Will you be gone long? I don't know how I'll be able to stay there without Mama being there."

"Naw. I shouldn't be long. An hour at the most."

"Okay."

I drove away from the curb and headed to Mama's house while Val silently cried. I hoped like hell she could get herself together this time, because if she didn't, I'd be burying her next.

❧

"So, after you got sent off to Navasota, I started doing lil small time shit. Lo thought I was killing the shit, so he kept me climbing the ladder. I'd lost my job and I needed to do something to make ends meet. My mama had been struggling after my dad died and I'd been helping her. Sky was involved in all kinds of shit in school. I couldn't let baby girl suffer while I tried to find something else. She was only eleven or twelve. So, I did what I had to do. After Lo got killed and Jeremy took over, he made me his right hand."

"I can't believe this shit. I would have never thought you was out here like this. How in the fuck you hid this shit from yo' mama and Sky?"

"Well, Sky was young. She didn't know any different. I ended up getting a job before Jeremy promoted me. Nobody noticed when I quit that shit. They always called my cell phone and I wore pants and a t-shirt to work, so I kept wearing that shit so they wouldn't ask questions. I stayed away from them when I was supposed to be at work. That shit was easy to pull off, especially since I didn't have nosy women in my life."

I shook my head slowly in amusement. That was probably why he came out here to Port Arthur to avoid running into him. "So, how did my name come up in the mix?"

"When you got out, he expected you to fall back in line. He thought you were gonna come work for him. I knew that wasn't gonna happen. I told him if you came back, it would be to claim your rightful place in this shit. So, when you didn't, he was relieved at first. But when he saw you making moves, he got jealous. He scoped out your family, trying to do shit to pull you back in. When someone broke in yo' mama house, that was him. He was also the one that got Val hooked on that shit. After that, he thought he had you. When you still didn't fold, he got desperate. I told him if you hadn't folded in all these years, you wouldn't fold now. But then he had me thinking you were in Houston running shit for some other nigga. That was why I didn't trust you at first."

"That muthafucka."

"Yeah. He was so damn jealous of you, it was pathetic. That nigga even went as far as to wanting to rob you. That shit threw me off. Because I hadn't seen you so much as even worried about his ass. So, I had a nigga start watching you after Sky broke things off with you. She was so heartbroken, and I hated seeing her like that. I'm already protective of her, because she's like *my* baby... my daughter instead of my sister. I needed to check Jeremy's story. Lying ass nigga."

I was still sitting there in disbelief. The only dealings I had with Jeremy was when it concerned Val. "That was some grimy, hating ass shit right there. I'm glad you decided to check it out for yourself."

"Yeah. Too much shit wasn't lining up with what he said. He'd started forgetting his own lies, but I was playing that shit smooth, not letting him know that I knew he was a jealous ass nigga."

"You are nothing like I thought you were at first."

He chuckled. "Naw. I can't have street Wes around my sister. I'm Weslan, the college dropout, big brother that took care of her and always looked out for her. This would break her heart."

"I think she may have an idea. She's been talking to Nikki."

"Yeah. That's why I'm going over there when we leave here," he said as he took a bite out of his boudin.

"She's cooking for me."

"Oh, yeah? She definitely loves you. My bad." He paused and held his hand at his chest. "I'm sorry about yo' mama."

"Thanks. So, what happened with Nikki?"

"That week in Galveston, Nikki met Jeremy on the beach. She and I had been talking, but we hadn't solidified what we were doing. We've known each other a long time and were friends, so it was kind of difficult to transition to more. When they came back, I knew something wasn't right about her. She wouldn't tell me what was going on, though. We became a couple that same week. About a week ago, she finally told me that he'd raped her. They had sex once, but the second time, another one of our guys joined them and she wasn't down with that shit. When she tried to leave, they both raped her. After she told me his name, I knew I was gon' take his ass out. I just had to set shit up to catch him alone."

"Who was the other nigga?"

"Some muthafucka named Terrence. I set his ass up to look like he drowned. That was light work. When I found out about your mama dying, I knew you would be coming for him. I couldn't let that happen. You ain't in this shit no more. So, now that he's gone, you shouldn't have anymore problems. Everyone knows not to sell shit to Val no more and that she isn't even allowed at none of the houses. I got'cho back. Now, I *was* uncomfortable with the age difference between you and my sister. I thought you were going after her for all the wrong reasons. Being with her just to see if you could pull a younger woman. But the heart wants what the fuck it wants."

I shook my head as I chuckled, then looked at the time. I'd been gone for an hour and I needed to get Val situated. "Well, I appreciate you, man. Thanks for looking out when it comes to Val, too. She gon' kill herself on that shit. I gotta get back to her before she disappear on me."

"A'ight. Well, I'll see you at Sky's house."

"A'ight, bruh."

He smiled at me calling him bruh as we slapped hands.

When I got to my mama's house, I blew the horn and prayed Val wasn't on no bullshit. After a couple of minutes, she came out with a duffle bag and I was grateful. My biggest fear as I drove here was that I would find her in the house dead from an overdose. She got in the SUV and smiled at me. "I thought I would be climbing the walls in there, but somehow it gave me a sense of comfort. It was like I could feel Mama's spirit in there. Like she was telling me it was alright and that she forgave me."

I smiled at her, something I hadn't done in years, and grabbed her hand. "Let's get you back to yourself, sis."

"Yeah. Let's do this, baby bro."

I kissed her hand and headed to Beaumont. If I thought I could trust her, I would have brought her to Sky's house. She'd taken a shower and she smelled okay, but crackheads were thieves. If she stole from Sky, I'd fuck her up. After we got to the Holiday Inn, I checked her in and carried her bag to her room. "I'll see you about noon. Okay?"

"Okay." She kissed my cheek and said, "Thank you."

My mama looked beautiful in her white dress. She looked like an angel. Val and I sat at the front of the funeral home, holding hands, and Sky sat to my left, holding my other hand. This was one of the hardest things I'd ever had to do. A few of our relatives were there, but I wasn't tripping about them. If they came, they came. Some of my managers and marketing people, as well as

Weslan and Nikki had shown up as well. When we were getting along at Sky's place the other night, she was happy, but questioning what had happened to change Weslan's mind about me. When he told her about Jeremy and that he was still smoking weed, she relaxed a little bit. He refused to tell her that he'd killed him.

We'd talked more that night, and he said he'd overdosed that nigga, too, and left a gun there to make it look like a suicide. Hopefully he did that shit right, because forensics didn't play. They'd figure that shit out quick. I was just glad that all of that was behind us. Although my mama was no longer here, I prayed that this was what it took to get Val on the right track. She'd finally confessed to me that Jeremy had actually been the one to break Mama's ribs. Taking the blame for everything was only right, she said. Had it not been for her bringing Jeremy there, Mama would still be alive.

When we got to the cemetery, the funeral director moved quickly as per my request. I didn't like prolonging shit for tradition. *Just say what you have to say so we can be done with this.* Val had held up well, and despite her skeletal figure, she looked nice. Whenever we left from here, we all planned to go to Cheddar's to eat. As we stood and prepared to get back in my SUV, several people hugged me and Val and offered well wishes. I walked to the casket and touched it, then pulled a flower from the spray. Thankfully, everyone left me alone so I could have a moment with her by myself. "I'm sorry it ended this way, Ma. I love you and I feel like you knew that. I'm gonna miss you. I did my best to make you proud after all the disappointment I caused you. Rest well."

When I turned around, I couldn't stop the tear that slid down my cheek. Sky was there to wipe it from my face, and Val hugged me tightly. Briefly closing my eyes, I took a deep breath and asked, "Y'all ready?"

Everyone nodded. I kissed Sky's lips, then grabbed her hand as we walked to the SUV. Once inside, Val said, "So, I go to rehab today or tomorrow?"

"Tomorrow. You can chill with us today, enjoy a sense of family."

"Thanks," she said softly.

I knew she was thinking about the road ahead, so I said, "One day at a time. Don't dwell on the long-term right now. Just focus on the current. Today. Before you know it, you'll be clean and sober for a year."

"You're right," she said, then took a deep breath. "Have you decided on a rehab?"

"Yeah. You'll be in Houston, close to me, so I can check on you."

I also wanted her away from the area, so they wouldn't arrest her. As long as she was doing right, I'd make sure she was free. As I looked at her in the rearview mirror, I saw a soft smile on her lips. Bringing Sky's hand to my lips, I kissed it twice, and continued to Cheddar's. Thinking on the funeral, I was glad that I was able to put my mama away with a little class, something she would never let me do for her while she was living. I could hear her voice in my head saying, *This shit is so damn bougie, Cole. I'm not one of those well-to-do white people. And I'm definitely not an uppity nigger, either. I'll be damn if I'm gon' look like one.* I shook my head slowly at the memory.

However, sitting at the funeral, that recollection made me more at ease and offered comfort to me. I saw what Val was talking about when she was at Mama's house the other night. She looked like an uppity nigga in that casket, and she deserved it. I just hated that she wasn't able to see it. I'd tried to give her her flowers while she could smell them, but she'd rejected her flowers. That was neither here nor there. The whole point was that she had a slight smile on her face like she was truly at peace. That was all I could ask for at the moment.

## ❧ 20 ❧

S ky

It had been a month since we'd buried Colson's mother and things had somewhat gone back to normal. We took turns visiting one another on the weekends, and it was his weekend to come to me. I'd been trying to be everything he needed me to be. It had taken me a while to move on from my mother's death. After taking an entire month off from work, I still wasn't ready to go back. I had to take a whole 'notha week just to get myself together. So, I was trying to be for Colson what I wished someone had been for me when my mama died. Weslan did his best, but he was grieving, too.

I was so grateful that he was finally okay with me and Colson's relationship. It was hard pulling away from my brother. When he saw how much being without Colson affected me, he eased up on me and took the time to get to know Colson. They seemed really close, now. Almost like best friends. That made me extremely happy. Although, I wasn't happy with how he tried to go after Jeremy. I had to tell him that I knew about it, because of what Nikki told me. But like Colson, he said he couldn't find him. I didn't know if they'd corroborated their story, or if one of them was lying, but neither were in jail or dead, so I accepted their responses without further questioning. We ended up enjoying dinner that night and promised to go on double dates occasionally.

I'd set up a massage table that I'd rented right in the front room and had a spa that I would do Colson's pedicure in. Colson deserved the world for everything he'd overcome in his life, and for his will to do better. He'd been pressuring me about moving to Houston, but he had yet to tell me he loved me, so I was holding off. Although he was pressuring me, it wasn't being done in a spiteful way or in a way to make me feel sorry for him. It was just through his statements of longing. Like him saying he wished he could wake up to me every day, or that he could hold me in his arms all the time.

If I applied pressure about him being in love with me, it wouldn't be genuine. We'd known one another for almost four months now, and things had been perfect. Besides when his mother died, we hadn't had any major drama since we'd gotten back together, and I felt that spoke volumes as to how perfect we were for one another. Hopefully, he would feel comfortable soon, to where he could tell me how he felt for me, because his actions showed it every day. If he wasn't sending me flowers at work, he was sending food or scheduling me for spa days. He said he refused to let the pressures of teaching those bad-ass kids pull me down any further. Thankfully, I only had half a week left until my summer vacation. For some stupid reason, I'd chosen to do the first session of summer school.

After putting the grilled steaks and baked potatoes in the oven to keep them warm, I lowered the fire on the snap beans. Colson loved beef meat. Because he worked out so often, he ate a lot of protein. I started doing the same thing and going to the gym. He'd explained that it was healthy for weight loss that a person ate a lot of protein. I'd lost about ten or fifteen pounds when he noticed. He'd asked with a frown on his face, *Why are you losing weight?* I'd chuckled in response. He thought I was stressed or something. When I'd told him what I was doing, he was impressed, but he'd also assured me that he loved the size that I was, and that if I loss too much weight, he'd have to ban me from the gym. I promised him that I only really wanted to tone up what I had. My legs were huge, and I wanted them to be a little toner than what they were.

After I'd gotten the oils set up by the table, I took a shower. Pulling my hair up into a bun, I moisturized every part of my body and put on a sexy silk robe. Colson loved for his first sight of me on the weekends to be of me naked. I'd done that, and for the most part, it resulted in us having sex before we did anything else. As I made my way back to the front, I heard the doorbell ring. A smile made its way to my face. Peeking through the peephole, seeing that it was him, I untied my robe and let it hang open. When I opened the door, he walked in, holding a bouquet of flowers as his eyes narrowed into slits as he stared at me sexily.

As soon as I closed the door, he pulled me to him and kissed my lips. "Hey, baby. You look good enough to eat."

"Hey, Colson. You look amazing, too."

I smiled because it was the same thing every weekend. He was always sure to compliment me every chance he got. After letting me go, he handed me the flowers, then walked further into the room, noticing the massage table. He frowned slightly, and looked back at me as I made my way to the kitchen to put my flowers in water. "What's the massage table for, baby? You wanted a massage?"

"No. You make sure I get those regularly. I wanted to give you a full body massage and a pedicure."

He gave me a one-cheeked smile. "I don't know if I'll be able to handle you rubbing on me like that, baby, without going further."

"We can go further after I finish."

"Naw. You probably won't finish. Secondly, you ain't finna rub on my feet, having me all sensitive and shit."

I slightly rolled my eyes as I finished playing with my flowers and washed my hands. When I opened the oven, Colson was standing behind me, holding me at my hips. "You may not even start. You know it's hell for me to resist the urge to feel your walls around me when I first get here."

"I know, baby. But let's at least eat first. I'll tie my robe, so you won't be tempted."

"You will do no such thing."

When I turned around to face him, his lips mated with mine, making sweet music as they always did. I loved him so much; I could barely function at times. Getting all the way lost in him was something I could see happening, and I didn't mind at all. After pulling away from me, he said, "Damn, I missed you."

"I missed you, too, baby."

Turning back to the oven, I took out our dinner and brought it to the stove as he followed me. "That looks good. I guess I can wait until after dinner," he said as he slid his blazer off.

I knew he was in a hurry to get to me, since he hadn't even taken his jacket off. Plating our food, I brought it to the bar where we always sat unless Weslan and Nikki joined us, then got our drinks. Once I sat, we blessed the food and dug in. His eyes closed as he took his first bite of the steak. "This is really good, baby."

"Thank you."

We continued eating, making small talk about our day, then I cleaned up while he took a shower. Usually we cleaned up together, but I thought we could get to the main attraction a little quicker if we did it this way. Colson didn't seem to have any objections. I told him when he came out not to be wearing anything, because he would be coming straight to the massage table. He gave me a smirk, but I was sure he would do as I asked. I poured myself a glass of wine and sipped as I turned on music from our playlist.

When that fine muthafucka walked down that hallway, I damn near came on myself. Just watching his big dick energy through his stride was enough to have me all discombobulated and flustered. My lips had parted as I watched all that swag approach me. His eyes were saying, *fuck that massage,* and my body was saying the same thing. But I couldn't flake on that. The pedicure could wait, though. He deserved a moment of relaxation... if I could make myself move. I'd been staring at him as he stood in front of me with a smirk on his face. *Shit!*

My eyes focused on his growing erection, then they slid back up to his face. "So, what we doing, Ms. Jones?"

I cleared my throat and broke my gaze away from his. "Umm... I need you to lay on this table. On your stomach first... if you can," I said as my eyes went back to his erection.

"I can lay on my stomach if I'm laying on you."

"On the table. Come on, baby. Let me give you this kingly treatment, big daddy."

"Big daddy, huh? Keep on. The only thing you gon' be massaging is this dick. But I'ma cooperate for a lil while."

He got on the table, then adjusted himself as he laid down, dropping his head to the face port. I lusted over his flesh for a moment... all that tight, caramel complexioned skin. His firm ass and muscled legs. *Jesus Christ.* I just wanted to lick him up... massage him with this tongue. It was like I was a different person whenever he was around. Grabbing the oil, I drizzled some on his back, while he laid there quietly. When my hands touched him, his skin reddened. I slid them up to his shoulders and kneaded his muscles there, then went to his neck.

I couldn't afford to stay in one spot too long, because I knew he would stop me. By the time I made my way to his legs, that was it. With one rub of his thighs, he turned over on his back, his slightly curved dick standing at attention. "Sky... the massage is over."

"Is it?" I asked, staring at the perfection that was beckoning me to it.

I grabbed his dick and began stroking it. His eyes closed, and he took a deep breath, slowly exhaling. As I stroked, I could see the pre-cum oozing from the head of his dick. Swiftly lowering my head, I licked it firmly, producing a groan from him. He sat up on his elbows as I licked the shaft and sucked on his balls, still stroking his dick with my hand. Making my way back up to his dick, he sat up completely. "This table ain't that stable. When I want that pussy, I want to be able to just pull you on top of me, baby."

He stood and grabbed me by the hand, pulling me down the hallway to my bedroom. My heart rate was creepin' on ah come up. *Colson would be happy with my Bone Thugs-n-Harmony reference.* I giggled silently. He'd been educating me musically. When we got to my bedroom, he swung me around to the bed and gently pushed me down, then put his dick on my lips. "Let's resume, baby."

I smiled and swallowed his shit whole as he grabbed a handful of my hair, slow stroking my mouth. My clit was protruding, and my nipples were hard, needing to be sucked on. They were throbbing, fiending for his touch. I moaned as his dick touched the back of my throat, threatening to go right down my food pipe. "Oh fuck."

I assume the vibrations from my vocal performance touched him in a way that he liked, because he put his other hand to my head and began fucking my mouth as he liked. I gagged quite a bit before he nutted right down my damn throat, filling me with that good protein, unattainable from anywhere else. He slowly slid his dick from my mouth, and laid on the bed on his back. "Shit. Come drown me, Sky."

When I straddled his face and got ready to lower myself to his lips, he said, "Mmm. That shit look like rain clouds. It's finna rain, baby?"

"Only if the rainmaker works his magic."

He didn't respond verbally. Roughly grabbing my hips, he pulled me to his lips and began speaking a language only I understood. I began to slowly grind on his face as he sucked my clit. "Oooh, Colson, shit."

Him squeezing my ass, then slapping it, made me grind faster. He took every bit of my bucking and shit with ease, slurping up my juices to try to satisfy his unquenchable thirst for all I had to offer. When he licked my shit, then pushed his stiffened tongue into my opening, my eyes rolled to the back of my head. I did that quite often whenever Colson was pleasing me. Some things he did to my body were just so overwhelming, no other action could express how much I loved the way he made me feel. He went back to my clit, and the moment he sucked it, I exploded all over him. "Fuuuck! Colson! Shit!"

As I tried to ease off him while my entire body shivered, he wrapped his arms around my legs and pulled me right back to him. He sucked the living daylights out of my pussy, and my orgasm wouldn't subside. That shit felt like it would be never ending. My clit was so fucking sensitive; I almost couldn't handle any more of his tongue. But with the grip he had on my thighs, I wasn't going anywhere. When he'd had his fill, he said against my pussy, "I love you."

I tried to pretend I didn't hear him. *Was he talking to her or me?* Instead of asking him, I remained quiet. He slid me off him as I panted, and he wiped his mouth. However, as I normally did when he hovered over me, I licked his lips. He gave me one of those nasty, 'I'm finna handle business' looks, then pushed inside of me. "Oh fuck!" he said in a low voice.

Nothing about the love I had for him was ordinary. He stroked me slowly and deeply as he licked at my nipple. He had me feeling like the most desirable woman in the world when he made love to me. I arched my back for a moment, then wrapped my thick legs around him. His pace remained steady as he slid his hand up my chest between my breasts to my neck. His fingers softly and slowly graced my cheek. When I opened my eyes for a moment, I found him staring at me. My breathing quickened even more so. His lips made their way to mine, and he kissed me softly, giving me his tongue.

It was the most sensual kiss he'd ever given me. He sucked my tongue as he pulled away from me. Once again, I opened my eyes to find his on me. Continuing to stroke me to ecstasy, he leaned his forehead against mine, then lifted my leg straight up. "Sky... shit. You feel amazing. Damn."

"So do you, babyyyyy," I said as my orgasm took ahold of me and wouldn't turn loose.

That shit came without its typical warning. As I came down from its effects, Colson gently rubbed my cheek again. We stared into one another's eyes as he deepened his stroke. The frown that adorned his face turned me on even more, because I knew my body was about to drain him of his nutrients. Biting his bottom lip, he began grunting, then let out a deep growl as he emptied his seed inside of me. When he'd settled some, he stared at me once again. *Just say it, Colson.* "Sky, I love you, baby."

My breathing went shallow as I stared at him. I'd been waiting months to hear him say that, and they were the most beautiful words he'd ever spoken to me. He stroked my cheek as a tear trickled down it. "I love you so much."

I bit my bottom lip for a moment and put my hand at the back of his bald head. "So, I have three more days of work. When do I move?"

# EPILOGUE

## Colson
### 1 year later...

IF I WOULD HAVE KNOWN THAT LOVE COULD FEEL THIS DAMN good, I would have told Sky long before I did. I just needed to know that I could trust her. After I admitted to her what she said she knew all along, I put some wheels into motion and had my assistant looking at listings in Katy. I didn't want to move Sky in my bachelor pad. Something more stable was needed to raise a family. Within a couple of weeks after my request, we were practically ready to close on a nice four-bedroom, two-story brick home.

Sky enjoyed the school district here a lot more than the one she'd currently been in, and it seemed to renew her drive to make a difference in the lives of her students. I was grateful for that, because I knew that she enjoyed teaching. Staying true to my word, I took care of everything financially. That was somewhat of a battle at first, but she swiftly gave in when I reminded her of what I told her would come with my love for her.

When I walked in the house, Sky was wobbling toward the fridge. She was due to deliver our first baby in a couple of weeks. We'd chosen to keep the baby's sex a secret. So, our excitement only grew with every passing week. She'd had a relatively smooth pregnancy with only the minor aches and pains that came with the territory. When she revealed her pregnancy to me, I was so damn excited, I called Weslan and Nikki and went got Val to go out for dinner.

Val was doing extremely well. She was living in a small apartment in Houston and working for me at Colson Furniture. She'd also gained a good sixty pounds since Mama died. I was proud of her. She'd said changing her environment was a big help to her, since she didn't know where to go to cop from. Houston was a lot more dangerous than Port Arthur, and she wasn't willing to die to get high. She came over almost every Sunday for dinner, and she and Sky had gotten close as well. "Hey, baby. How you feeling?"

"Hey, Colson. I've been having quite a bit of pressure, but I'm okay."

"You sure? We can go to the hospital."

"I'm sure."

"Well, come sit down, baby, and put your feet up. At least the baby is full-term now. I'm excited as hell."

"I'm excited, too," she said as she kissed my lips. "How was your day?"

"It was good. I was just anxious for it to pass so I could get back to you."

She smiled softly at me as she sat in the recliner and I lifted her feet. They were good and swollen, and her nose had spread. But I never heard her complain. She was so excited to be having a beautiful baby. I knew there was one thing she was waiting on, though. We wanted to get married. I wished we would have done it a long time ago, but she wanted to plan out something intimate, but extravagant. She said she needed a few months to look at everything and decide on a wedding planner that would be able to deliver what she wanted.

Once we found out she was pregnant, she slammed on the brakes. She didn't want to be pregnant when we got married. By the date she was thinking about setting, she would have been six months pregnant. I didn't realize just how bougie her tastes were until we moved in together. "What did you want to eat, baby?"

"Nikki and Weslan are on their way out, and they said they would bring dinner."

"Oh. What are they bringing?"

"Nikki did some ox tails, but I don't remember what sides."

"A'ight. Sounds like a plan. I'm gonna go take a shower, then."

Weslan and Nikki were engaged as well and were scheduled to get married sometime next year. Weslan was still running the streets of Port Arthur as far as I knew and had managed to keep it a secret from Sky. I wasn't sure whether Nikki knew about it or not. Just as I took my clothes off and was about to get in the shower, Sky screamed, "Colson! Get my bag out the closet! My water just broke!"

I damn near broke my damn neck trying to run back in the room to put some clothes on. Throwing on some basketball shorts and a t-shirt, I slid into my Nike slides and grabbed her bag from the closet floor. When I made my way back to her, I sat the bag on the table, then helped her out of her bottoms. Running back to the room, I got her some underwear and a pair of maternity pants. When I made it back to her, she was slumped in the chair. "Come on, baby. Let's get these on you and we'll go."

Helping her stand, she held onto me as I got her dressed, then I threw the duffle bag over my shoulder and picked her up, carrying her to the SUV, so I could bring her to Texas Women's Hospital. Once I got her in and buckled up, I hauled ass and realized we weren't going to make it. We were right in the midst of traffic. *Shit!* I took her to Methodist West Campus here in Katy and prayed that her doctor would come there. If not, I was sure that someone there was capable of bringing our baby into the world safely.

Sky had screamed a couple of times, scaring the shit out of me, because she'd had some pretty hard contractions. Once we got there and I was carrying her in, a nurse came with a wheelchair and raced her to the labor and delivery floor. As they took her to a room, I had to hang behind to give them information. I also called Weslan to let him and Nikki know where we were. When I walked in the room, the nurses had gotten Sky undressed and hooked to a monitor. They were getting her IV setup, and another was about to do an exam to see how far she'd dilated. I quickly texted Val, then stood next to Sky and grabbed her hand. "Baby, I'm scared."

"Don't be. We've been waiting for this moment. I'm gonna be here every step of the way. Weslan and Nikki are on their way." Grabbing my phone to look at the text I'd received from Val, I said, "And so is Val."

The nurses helped her lift her legs to the stirrups and one of them said, "Oh my. The baby is coming now! The head is starting to crown."

Right after, Sky screamed. "Oh God! It's too late for pain medicine! Colson, what am I gonna do?"

"You gon' handle this like you handle everything else. You got this, baby."

The doctor burst into the room with his hands in the air, and a nurse was pushing a cart. It was so many people in the room, they were making me nervous. I couldn't let Sky see my nerves, though. She was nervous enough on her own. "Okay, Ms. Jones. We're ready when you are. When you feel the next contraction, I need you to push with all your might."

Sky nodded as her grip on my hand tightened. She began pushing, screaming and crying while doing so, and within seconds, the baby's head was already out. When she'd felt that pressure earlier, she was in labor and didn't even know it. "Okay. Stop, Ms. Jones. One more push and you should be done. Next contraction."

I rubbed her head as she turned to me. I kissed it just as her next contraction ripped through her. She pushed with all her might, and the baby slid right out of there, screaming and crying. "It's a boy, Ms. Jones!"

I smiled big as they handed me the scissors to cut the umbilical cord. Sky looked overjoyed as well as she stared at our baby boy. They laid him on her chest as she cried and gently stroked his head with her fingers. I kissed her cheek and looked at our beautiful son. "Colton Rondel Crook," she said looking at me.

"I love it, baby."

She could have named him whatever she wanted, and I would have been okay with it. The point was that God had finally saw fit to bless me with a son. And within a few months, I would have a wife.

*The End*

# AFTERWORD

From the Author

These two characters right here had my pressure up a lil bit. LOL Not only them, but the supporting characters as well. Colson and Sky were extremely compatible and I loved them together. I hope you did as well.

There's also an amazing playlist on iTunes for this book under the same title that includes some great R&B and rap tracks to tickle your fancy. Please keep up with me on Facebook (@authormonicawalters), Instagram (@authormonicawalters) and Twitter (@monlwalters). You can also visit my Amazon author page at www.amazon.com/author/monica.walters to view my releases. Also, subscribe to my webpage for updates! https://authormonicawalters.wixsite.com/mysite.

For live discussions, giveaways and inside information on upcoming releases, join my Facebook group, Monica's Romantic Sweet Spot at https://bit.ly/2P2lo6X.

Be Careful What You Wish For

You Just Might Get It

Show Me You Still Want It

### Sweet Series

Bitter Sweet

Sweet and Sour

Sweeter Than Before

Sweet Revenge

Sweet Surrender

Sweet Temptation

Sweet Misery

Sweet Exhale

### Motives and Betrayal Series

Ulterior Motives

Ultimate Betrayal

Ultimatum: #lovemeorleaveme, Part 1

Ultimatum: #lovemeorleaveme, Part 2

### Written Between the Pages Series

The Devil Goes to Church Too

The Book of Noah (A Crossover Novel with The Flow of Jah's Heart by T Key)

The Revelations of Ryan, Jr. (A Crossover Novel with All That Jazz by T Key)

CPSIA information can be obtained
at www.ICGtesting.com
Printed in the USA
LVHW111600051120
670844LV00003B/454